Pearls

To heck with Hawthorne,
O'Henry, and Poe;
My Turn at Bat

26 Great Short Stories

Pearls

Bill Monks

JJ COMPANY NEW YORK

First Printing 2002

©2001 Bill Monks. All Rights Reserved.

Library of Congress Catalog Number 2001132622
ISBN 0-9675915-2-X

Published by John James Company New York, NY

Printed in the United States of America

Contents

The Raccoon

I threw my bag on the rack above the seat and introduced myself to a well-dressed stranger; it was to be a seven-hour trip and there was no point in not being sociable.

"Bill Kias, heading up to Quantico." I offered my hand as I took my seat.

"Jack Funz from Alexandria." We sat quietly for a moment.

"Bill Kias, you say you're on your way to Quantico?"

"Yep, my son is a instructor at the FBI Academy, Where did you say you were bound for Jack, Alexandria? I hear that's a big steel town now."

"That's right. I'm with American Steel. I'm just coming back from Hamburg. I was over there trying to convince the Germans to let us erect an A.S. plant there."

"Do you speak the language? Gad, you couldn't look more Nordic." My companion had blond hair and the bluest eyes: they were actually sky blue. A very handsome chap. He looked like the type that Hitler thought of as supermen.

"No way, I'm third generation American. My great grandparents came from Milan. The original name is Funziano. There are a lot of blond Italians in northern Italy. But me, I'm from south Philly. I grew up there. I left when I went to Villanova."

Dinner hour approaching, I suggested that we retire to the dining car and eat our way through Mississippi. At dinner we discovered that we both had a weakness for Manhattans.

"I'll tell you something Bill, today most bartenders don't know how to make a good Manhattan. Where the hell is it going to end?"

"You know, Jack, to hell with saving the Yellow Belly Sapsucker. Who's looking after the Manhattan?" It's odd when strangers meet on a cruise ship, train, or in any spot where they are no longer connected to their roots. They grab hold of a freedom that permits them to speak from the heart. As the train rolled up the East Coast corridor, night had fallen. It was a pleasant dinner; I enjoyed Jack's company. It turned out we had a lot in common. We both had taken an active part in our church and had large families. I had just retired and he was about to. We both had served in the Pacific Theater. We exchanged the humorous and tragic incidents that make up family life. We both agreed that with large families, nothing passes by your door. You are condemned by the law of averages to experience everything.

"Bill, I would sit at the dinner table with the family and know that a broken leg, a wrecked car, drugs, and possibly an early death was paused outside my door. The card to each child had been dealt, but face down."

"You know Jack, I always felt the same way. The only surprise would be to whom it happened. You knew it was going to happen. That damn law of averages could not be repealed. Strange, I never realized how other parents must fear that law."

Jack was extremely proud of his family; he whipped out their pictures. Every one, including his wife, was blond. He shared a little about each one of his six children. Two of his sons had graduated from Harvard and were now lawyers, his daughter Meg, an astrophysicist. He had lost Jack Jr, shot down over Vietnam. His youngest son, who had left home at 18, was now serving a prison term.

Jack won my respect when he mentioned his son being in prison. That takes more than a Manhattan. Of course I also responded by sharing how life was in the chaos of the Kias family. We had seven kids, plus Vinn, a young man who was one of the Vietnamese boat people. Vinn lived with us for about 8 years.

"Jack, one day it occurred to me I wasn't the head of a household, I was the manager of an insane asylum. When the inmates heard me refer to the house as the asylum they gave me a white orderly's uniform for my birthday. I wore it and added a strait-jacket to the clothes in our hall closet.

"Over a period of thirty years, I had to make 22 trips to the Emergency Room without ever laying a hand on them. I got so tired of taking them to the hospital to have their casts removed that I learned how to do it myself. Once you get the hang of it, it's not too difficult.

"I always laugh when I think of how Vinn was introduced to the

American culture via the Kias family. I'm sure we left him with strange ideas about how the average American lives. He taught all the boys how to kick-box and everybody loved his cooking. I always had to keep an eye on the dog. He thought Trapper looked delicious.

"Vinn would sit on his haunches in the middle of the living room, watching TV. He always reminded me of those guys you would see down on their haunches, hands tied at the edge of the trail. I think they were waiting to be interrogated before they tossed them out of a helicopter.

"He would never let us throw out anything. He was real handy; he made us very conscious of how much we waste in this country. He could jury rig a watch. A real good boy, but God, was he inscrutable. To this day I can't decide whether he was Vietcong or an all right guy. When he first came, we had a kind of Inspector Clouseau, houseboy relationship. I would always sleep with one eye open, a trick I learned in the Corps.

"In the space of five years, he had his own business. I remembered how he was always shipping mysterious packages to Paris."

After dinner, Jack and I returned to our seats. Late into the night we exchanged tales of grief and humor, personal thoughts that I'm sure we had never discussed with another. Jack could tell a story.

It was as if for once we could bury all subterfuge and speak freely, nothing to sell and nothing to buy. It was more than kindred spirits. We had risen above our egos. We were just two strangers taking a risk, drawing the curtain and using this interlude to finally lay it all out. This went on for several hours.

"Bill, I'm sure you noticed my eyes. I have the damnedest bluest eyes. They always attracted attention. You'll enjoy this story; it's about those eyes and a lot more. You will be the first person I ever told it to, beside my priest. It happened thirty years ago. The story is fascinating, but you'll understand why I never told it to anyone."

"Jack, you're right about your eyes. They put Paul Newman's to shame. I noticed them the moment we met."

"So. One night, I'm working late at the office. I don't know if I told you, but I'm the Treasurer of American Steel. At that time I had to put some mean nights in, making up the budget. Most nights I would be alone till about eleven, then I would pack it in and head home.

"This one night I look up from my desk distracted by a young girl emptying my wastebasket. Bill, she was without doubt the most beautiful girl I had ever seen. Long jet-black hair, eyes that matched the ebony of her hair, a form divine. Her skin was that beautiful olive. She had that face that the Greeks appreciate.

"Each night she would come in for a brief moment, finish her task and leave. After a while I began to look forward to her entrance. I guess it started with a smile. I attempted to establish a relationship, only to find out, by sign more than anything else, that she was a native of Peru, and spoke no English.

"One night I invited her to join me at my desk, to share my coffee. I don't know how we communicated, but we did. She told me that she came from a small village, high up in the Andes and had just arrived in the U.S. She was captivated by my blond hair. She said I would be considered a god in her village. What really made her spellbound were my eyes. She had never seen eyes that color. As we would sit there I realized that my eyes had a magnetic hold on her. She looked at me as if I was actually a god.

"Well, it got to be a regular routine, the desk bit. I started teaching her English. I thought of it as a harmless break. But unknowingly I was becoming very attracted to her. I began thinking of her as my Inca Princess and I knew she was thinking of me as a god.

"Bill, I never fooled around in my life, in fact I had no respect for any idiot that did. This whole thing was crazy and getting out of hand. As the days went on I found her lurking in my mind. Vera didn't notice, but my princess was definitely hurting my marriage. One day I was determined to change my office to a different floor. As I was cleaning out my desk, she arrived early that evening.

"'Mr. Jack, Saturday, I go to Cleveland to my brother. I will not see you again.' Tears were in her eyes.

"Instead of a feeling of great relief, my stomach turned. My Inca Princess was leaving. All reason fled. God, I was in love with her. Like a fool I asked her to join me Friday evening for dinner at a nearby restaurant. I just wanted to say goodbye.

"'Honey, the fellows in the office have invited me out to bowl Friday. I'll be a little late. I don't even feel like going, but you know, you have to play the game.'

"'Jack, that sounds like a nice time. You certainly deserve some relaxation. Maybe you should join their league. All work no play.'

"Bill, for the next two days my conscience was eating me alive. I no longer felt at home in my own house. I found myself avoiding Vera. This kind of crap was new to me. How do guys do it? I kept telling myself, it's only one crummy night. The Princess and I will just have a drink and dinner and that's it. Who's to know? Who's to hurt? Vera said I deserved some relaxation.

"Friday night finally arrived. Well, you know what happens. I didn't make history. It starts off with hand holding at dinner and it ends up at two A.M. in a fleabag.

"I really blew it. God, I felt like garbage. Everything I valued and took pride in was gone. I wanted to drive the car into a tree. I tell you Bill; I had really despised any married man who was unfaithful. I convinced myself, 'She's gone, it's all over, it never happened. Vera will never know. Everybody is allowed one slip.'

"Quietly as possible, I pull the car into the driveway. I'm surprised to see the living room light still on. God, she waited up for me. While hanging my coat in the vestibule I hear her call.

"'Honey you're rather late. Did you have a good time? I hope you remembered your ulcer. Take a glass of milk and bring me a warm one, I just couldn't sleep.' She glanced up from her book as I entered. Her glance froze into horror, as I handed her the milk. 'JACK! JACK! What happened? My God Jack, you look horrible. What happened to you!' She was now on her feet, milk spilt.

"I thought, "What in hell is she talking about?" I quickly ran into the bathroom, in search of a mirror. Staring at me was the head of a man with the eyes of a giant raccoon. My Inca Princess had poured out her emotions on my eyes. I suddenly recalled her constant kissing of my eyes. I was a dead man."

"Jack, how in heaven's name did you get out of it?" I asked.

"Bill, how in hell could I get out of it? I racked my brain. I had to come up with an explanation. There wasn't any! Should I stonewall it? Deny any knowledge of the condition of my eyes?

"As I stared into the mirror I saw tears filling those horrible eyes. No. There would be no denial. I had had it. There was only one way back. I was going to tell the truth. God, I was going to tear Vera's heart out. It was going to be the hardest thing I ever did. There really wasn't a choice.

"As I stepped out of the bathroom, Vera was waiting for me, still with that alarmed face, and even more bewildered by my tears. I told her everything.

"Bill, It was the most passionate moment of our marriage. I sunk to my knees and wept, as I buried my head in her robe. My remorse was overwhelming. I was taking the sin and guilt and laying it at the feet of my innocent Vera. Bill, It is a strange thing to say, but honest to God, I felt as if I was at the foot of the cross, asking Him to forgive me. Vera stood silently with her small hands resting on my head. I don't know how long I knelt there weeping, but suddenly I felt the light kisses of Vera on my horrible eyes. She was kneeling, holding my face in her hands. 'Jack, I'll always love you. I am your wife.'"

"You dumped on her Jack. Never should have told her."

"Bill, that's just what my priest said."

"ALEXANDRIA! ALEXANDRIA! ALEXANDRIA!"

"That's for me Bill. Look out the window: you'll see Vera."

The Know-It-All Society

There were forty of us dining in the Russian Tea Room in New York. Each year we would gather for a dinner and a lecture given by a member of our legal department. Instead of the bank paying us overtime, they would give us a chicken dinner and beat us out of a few bucks.

I became aware of a strange phenomenon after I attended several of these dinners. Listening to the tone of the conversation, one could correctly surmise that there was a uniform difference of opinion. It wasn't as if one group opposed another. No, it was unique; all individuals opposed one another. It was similar to that old fable, where blind men, not knowing they are touching a different part of an elephant, attempt to describe the animal to one another. Even though their jobs at the bank were identical, none of them could agree on the proper procedures to follow. There was a constant hum of bickering, not an atmosphere for bonding. Why this uniform animosity among strangers? Why this abnormal behavior?

We all had the same occupation and worked for the same bank; our occupation had placed us in isolation. Each of us managed a safe deposit facility in one of the many branches of the bank and answered to no one. We were in absolute control of our environment. The bank's administration had completely neglected us. We spent our days alone in a hole in the ground and our customer contact was almost nil. Whatever we thought and formed an opinion of, became our truth. Opinion is only an opinion as long as it is open to questioning. If the opinion is not questioned it becomes the truth. If you live or work in an isolated condition, you have no opinions, you just know.

The isolated conditions had created gods by default. Living in our solitude it was as if we talked to ourselves and found that we were not only an interesting speaker but we were convinced we spoke the

14

truth. As time passed, we left no room for debate. We developed absolute faith in our beliefs; they had become facts.

The bank manual governing the precepts of safe deposit departments had been long out of date. Whatever legal controls over estates and different forms of businesses were to be in effect, was determined by what each hermit decided was right. The manual was no longer consulted.

Existing in isolation, you are quite content and harmless. In fact, your self-esteem tends to grow to a degree that you bow to no man. You are not aware that you have been subjected to a syndrome that can have a dire effect on those who share your company. Your attitude and behavior painfully hampers assimilation in your community. The results of this syndrome can lead to the breakup of marriages and painful living conditions for children.

After noting this strange behavior at these dinners, I recalled a test the Navy conducted in Antarctica after WWII. They placed a group of volunteers in isolated huts for a period of a year. They were secluded from all human contact. The operation was conducted to determine what effect total isolation would have on a human. They were given all sorts of psychological tests before and after their prolonged solitude. It was found that a singular personality change had taken place in each individual. During each session with the psychiatrist the volunteer spoke with authority, no matter what subject was being discussed. Each man was confident that what he said was true without question. They had become "Know-It-Alls."

I realized that this was exactly what we were unknowingly suffering from. We were victims of too much time in the vault, or vault syndrome. This syndrome will strike at any person who lives a life of isolation or works at a job that does not call for social contact. Those suffering from this syndrome can be easily detected. They are constantly referred to as a "Know-It-All" by their spouses and associates. Certain idioms in their speech give them away: "I beg to differ," "Not so," "Bullshit," "Do you really want to know?" They also have a tendency to finish a statement with the phase: "You better believe it." The "Know-It-All" tends to be drawn to discussion clubs. Being a "Know-It-All," I have always enjoyed a good controversy and have a gift for pontificating.

When I realized my audience was thinning I placed an add in the local paper announcing the formation of the "Know-It-All Society." The goal of the organization was to gather our most brilliant men in the community into a discussion group. We were to seek out and solve the multiple problems of mankind. It was to be a society that would meet each month to discuss a volatile subject drawn out of a hat. The only requirement for membership was to be a member of that rare breed of "Know-It-Alls." If you had any doubts that you qualified for membership, you were to consult with your family and associates.

The motto of K.I.A.S. is "nothing sacred". All subjects, including creation, politics, philosophy, religion, abortion, marriage, divorce, children, the cosmos, woman's lib, sports, or any topic that might bring the blood to a boil and a temper to flair, was open game. We use the time between meetings to sharpen our expertise on the subject to be discussed. We are there to exchange truths; any one who uses the phrase "that is my opinion" is labeled an ignoramus and quickly weeded out.

The response of both men and woman to the ad was so favorable that we had to change the location of the meeting place from my home to local restaurants. I use the plural because quite often we are asked to leave. Up to now no one has been seriously hurt. The town has gotten into the habit of having a police car parked in the vicinity of our meeting.

We realized at our first get together that Robert's Rules would hamper and slow the pace of the discussion. We settled on one rule, and we do insist on its enforcement. You can't kick or stomp on a member while he or she is down.

When we were first founded we would start the meeting off with a guest speaker. Now we just can't get them. They all seemed to have the same problem. They can't handle the question period at the close of their talk. We all agreed that they didn't know what the hell they were talking about anyway.

When K.I.A.S. (it's pronounced 'chaos') held it's first presidential election, we had rather a unique problem. The ballot box disclosed that it was a dead tie. Each member had voted for himself. We then had to devise a system that would not allow for a tie and yet permit each member the opportunity to serve. We decided that the last person standing would be the most qualified for the office. On election night the town's Paddy wagon replaces the patrol car.

The President has only one responsibility and that is to maintain proper decorum. Proper decorum is understood to be any behavior that is short of kicking and stomping.

If you think you are of the right stuff and wish to come to one of our meetings, let me tip you off to our password: "Bullshit," and keep your left out.

The Ark

The occupation of Chichi Jima after WW II had come to a close; we were finally ordered to return to Guam. We had sent all Japanese troops back to their mainland, all except the prisoners. Chichi was to be placed in a U.N. Trusteeship and the island was to be uninhabited for the next twenty years. Our orders of departure contained the strange request that all livestock on Chichi were to return with us.

The livestock consisted of 19 horses; numerous pigs, goats, chickens, dogs and one monkey named Hojo. Hojo was a member of Charlie Co. He had joined Charlie during the Bougainville campaign. The Colonel had been using the horses found on the Island to whip some of the farm boys into the first and last Marine Corps cavalry outfit. Being a gentleman from Virginia, he knew his horses and something about cavalry drills.

The vessel we were to return on was small. The ship was a Landing Ship Tank, or LST, mainly used during the war as a landing craft for troops and armor. The ship was 300 ft. in length with a beam of 50 ft. and a crew of 110. It was 1,625 tons with a flat bottom. Most striking were the large doors that made up its bow. When the craft ran up on the beach these huge doors would open, then like a large tongue, a ramp would come out of the open mouth. Tanks and troops would then spew out onto the beach. I give you all these details because in the following yarn the ship is the main character.

We loaded our strange cargo into the hold, and made them as comfortable as we could among the trucks, jeeps and the rest of our supplies. The situation did not look too promising for our four legged sailors. We constructed a wooden shack on the main deck to act as a brig for our Japanese prisoners. These men were being taken back to Guam to stand trial for war crimes.

After a day out at sea, the smell of the animals permeated the ship. We were sailing in a dirty barn. It was painful trying to sleep amid the grunting of the pigs, the barking of the dogs, the baa of the goats and the neighing of the horses. We had a regular Spike Jones band below deck. Chickens were starting to wander around the deck.

The second night out, the ship started taking a beating from a heavy sea. We received word that a typhoon was about to bear down on us and to secure everything. How do you secure a zoo?

A sailor told me that prior to the ship's arrival at Chichi they had lost their regular Captain, who had been transferred to another ship. An inexperienced Executor Officer was now the Acting Captain and the crew did not trust him. The executive was about to get his baptism of fire. Within a couple of hours, the wind velocity had increased to 70 mph. I recently consulted the U.S. Weather Bureau for the WD SP of that typhoon in that longitude & latitude during late March, 1946. They sent me a printout, that read, 045, 070, 070, 100, 085, 080, 090, 090. As any old swabbie would tell you, that was a blow and a half.

The ship was being tossed and battered in an honest to God typhoon. I stood out on the deck to watch the magnitude and power of the seas. I could actually see the ship bending amidships. The deck plates were continuously crying out in pain. A sailor reassured me that the ship was made to buckle amidships so that it wouldn't snap in half. I felt like crying along with the plates. The ship tipped more then rolled because of its flat bottom, on a good tip you could look UP at the sea. The decks were constantly awash.

WHOOSH! The brig we made for our prisoners went bottom up and blew over the side, leaving the Japanese still on the deck. We ushered them below deck. Our intentions were to hang them, not drown them. They must have had some fun in that shack while the ship pitched.

We were to be in the typhoon for several days. We were notified that the port on Guam was closed and to ride out the storm as best we could. I had been in rough weather before but nothing like this. The bow would ride high into the air and then come crashing down to bury itself in the sea. Prior to the storm, a sailor had informed me that the doors were damaged and had been jury-rigged to stay closed. I prayed they would.

The huge seas controlled our course. The ship appeared helpless as the helmsman's mettle was being tested, trying to keep the bow into waves in order to keep the ship from broaching. As we left Guam to our stern, the storm increased in velocity. It looked as if we were going to be blown as far south as Truk, in the Caroline Islands. Our brother Regiment, the 21st Marines who were stationed there, might be in for a surprise.

I was scared stiff. I wished that I hadn't heard about the doors or the inexperienced Executive. I always hated a rough sea, but this was like being in a blender.

As you would expect our sailors in the hold were taking heavy casualties. A lot of the poor animals, including several horses had died early on. The dead horses had bloated. The ship reeked from the smell of the dead and the waste of those still alive. This pungent aroma and the ferocity of the storm called for an iron stomach.

We were out at sea far longer then we had expected and therefore had to ration our chow and fresh water, not that anybody had an appetite. Marines and Sailors alike would just lie in their sacks with their head in their helmets, The helmets were strapped to the edge of the sacks and at night, as the ship tipped, you would hear the splashing on the deck, as the helmets ran over.

Some Marines volunteered to go into the hold and hoist out the dead horse carcasses through the main hatch. We all watched as the first horse, hog-tied, went out of the hold. The horse was bloated to twice its normal size and swinging like a pendulum. Just as the carcass was about to clear the hold, it broke in half, deluging the working party below, with horse. The audience fell on the deck laughing. Due to a shortage of volunteers, that work detail was canceled.

All day long the carcass of the horse followed in our wake. Was the mangled equine stalking us? It was positively eerie, was it horse or albatross? A blanket of gloom covered the ship.

I thought of the lines of Coleridge:

> And having once turned round, walks on,
> And turns no more his head;
> Because he knows a frightful fiend
> Doth close behind him tread.

The following morning our spirits rose as we finally escaped the storm and headed back to Guam; our pursuer had sunk beneath the waves. As we entered the harbor we breathed a sigh of relief, but it was much too soon. The Executive was about to dock a ship for the first time. If there is any sort of cross wind, combined with the loss of headway, docking can be a very difficult task for any seaman.

As we bore in, the Marines on board were lining the rail checking out the ships in the harbor. We appeared to be closing on a beautiful yacht, the "Lonely Lady," that was tied up to the pier. The sailors, pointing out its flag, told us it belonged to the Commodore of the Island. The yacht was J.P. Morgan class. It was a luxurious showpiece made of wood; its polished brass and varnished deck glistened in the sun. The only person on deck was a young officer, waving to us in a friendly manner, a very cool character. This guy seemed real smug; he knew he had it made. He looked like Ensign Pulver from that play Mr. Roberts: a ninety-day wonder, in new, neatly pressed khaki. His demeanor quickly changed to panic as he realized we had lost headway and were being blown into his side. He started making signs with his hands as if to push us off. It was now obvious we were about to mash the Lonely Lady against the dock. The guy on the yacht deck had by now completely lost it. He was springing into the air, waving his arms and screaming foul language. We came along broadside and tucked the Lonely Lady into the side of the pier.

The Marines were howling with laughter as we watched the polished planks pop and spring into the air. We kissed her, un-puckered and impolitely continued on our way. We had done extensive damage. We never exchanged a word with the maniac; he was not making any sense. This poor guy was in deep trouble with the Commodore. (Officer of the Deck, what deck?) As we proceeded deeper into the harbor, the sailors were cursing the Executive, and the Marine laughter could not be contained.

We were now heading for a docking space between two other LSTs, who had their doors open on to the beach. Sitting ducks! There was about a thirty-yard space between them.

I figured by now that every sailor in the harbor had his glasses trained on us and we didn't let them down. The docking operation looked to us as easy as parking a car. I'm sure it appeared that way to the Executive. As we approached the gap between the two ships, we slowed our forward motion and again we lost headway. The crosswind caught our bow, crashing us into the stern of the LST on our starboard side. As we backed off, we proceeded to cream the other ship on our port side with our stern.

We were on the verge of being wedged laterally between them. Nobody had the heart to laugh anymore; by now the Marines were bonded to our ship and we were sharing our shipmates' embarrassment. We could no longer even look.

Finally the three crews fought us free and we eventually docked between the ships. Our sailors wanted to take the ship back out to sea and go down with it. They all agreed that it would not be wise to take shore leave. The other two crews were complaining about a horrible smell.

We no longer noticed it; we have become the smell. Now came the *piece de resistance*. When the ship was made snug to the beach, the Exec gave the order, "Open the bow doors." Sure enough, with all the eyes of Guam staring at us, out of the mouth of our ship comes one hell of a bad breath, followed by the survivors of the typhoon: sick chickens, thin pigs, smelly goats, wild dogs, and a bunch of lame horses. Looking into the hold one can see a bloated horse has commandeered the Col.'s Jeep.

Hojo had been quartered with us, and was in the pink.

I want to know how the heck the Executive got us through that typhoon. I never saw the man. He is now probably living out in Kansas, far from the briny deep.

Next day the headline of the Guam Daily read:

NOAH'S ARK LANDS ON GUAM

The View

"Martha, this is the largest quilting bee we have had since the men left. Did you notice not having the men around has cut down on the quality of gossip? This will be the third fourth of July that they have been gone. I remember when my three boys left, they promised they be back by the following Independence Day; well tomorrow will be the third Independence Day that they have been away."

"I fear the war is not going well. They have been away too long. I heard the losses at Fredericksburg were horrible.

"In Ezra's last letter he said the Twentieth Maine were heading into Pennsylvania. That's on the way home isn't it? Maybe the three of them will show up for the parade tomorrow. Now wouldn't that patch the quilt?"

"Sara is so mad she said that if Josh don't come home soon, she is going to have her eye out for another man to marry. She is worried sick."

"Not likely Hinabel. I know she doesn't mean it, but every man worth marrying is gone from the village. I don't know how we managed to gather in the largest potato crop ever in any Maine county. All the youngens pitched in and did a fine job, but we need our men. Hasn't been a child born in this village in over a year. Jacob and Ezra were supposed to have helped Josh clear our south forty by now. Josh is planning to build a house over looking it, on that pretty little knoll. I don't know what got into those boys heads, to go off like that."

"Martha, I think some went for the fun of it, others because they were ashamed not to go, but most of them went because it was the right thing to do. Men will be boys."

"Know what I think Martha, I think it was that Colonel Chamberlain. He got our men whipped up about the Union and slavery. None of us has ever seen a slave. They thought they would be back before the seed potatoes went down. Didn't they look grand when they marched out of the village? They elected my Hiram, Captain. I don't really know why my husband went with six youngens at home. But I know he isn't coming back. Lucy's boy Zeb saw him get blown to pieces at Fredericksburg."

"What do they call this hill, Ezra? No peak to it, just a round top."

"I have no idea Jacob. What a beautiful view, much better land than we had at home.

"The birds have come back. There is a hawk circling over the peach orchard. Not that many stonewalls around, that means easy farming. Look at that wheat field, wouldn't we like to have that at home. On second thought Jacob, I could never stomach a piece of bread from that field. I would always taste the blood.

"Every once in a while I think I smell the peach blossoms from the orchard. You can't see the ground for the bodies. Look at that Reb and Yank lying there yonder, they look like their still fighting, both wrapped in that flag. We don't hate each other. It's our damn pride that turns us into killers. No animal on earth is more inhuman than man. Pride, our greatest sin kills us, not the Reb.

"You see that brick building with the cupola standing off to the right? The Colonel said that's a Lutheran seminary, that's where we first ran into them yesterday afternoon.

"Are you OK, Jacob?"

"Sure Ez, as long as I can sit here with this old tree supporting my back and my knees bent, I'm OK. We had one hell of a day. Would you look at the size of those boulders down there in the Devil's Den, some of them are darn near as big as our barn. There is no cover between them and us. While the Alabama boys are taking a breather, their snipers are playing hell with us. I'd be happy if we never saw them again, this side of hell. That yell is straight out of hell, I have never got used to it. When you get home Ezra, ask Mother to always keep two empty chairs at the table for us. Josh would like that. With Josh and me gone it's going to be a chore to clear the south forty. I guess there isn't going to be much new land cleared after this. Half our village went down today. We are going to miss another Fourth of July. Remember the barrel of fish chowder mother would prepare for the feast, after the races. I can still hear the violin that old McAfee played. Couldn't he make that violin cry, with those sad songs about his Ireland? I remember I asked Sara to marry me while he was playing The Bells of Cork. Ezra, don't tell Sara how I died. God how I loved her. We had dreams: our house on the hill, the children. Oh Sara I'm so sorry, forgive me. Ezra, I'm only twenty-two. What did mother always say? 'If you want to hear the good Lord laugh, tell him your plans.' Do you think it will ever end? Well it's over for me."

"Don't talk Jacob, just rest. We sure enough showed those boys today that Maine men are a stubborn lot. Those Rebs just kept coming. They wanted this hill as much as we did. Some of them call themselves 'the Louisiana Tigers.'

"This hill is soaked in blood, yet we couldn't grow a potato on it, nor they grow cotton or fish for scrimp. Both our states are a thousand miles from here.

"Who is going to run in the Fourth of July races? I really enjoyed that, especially beating Big Matthew every year. I wonder if anybody will ever top Big Matthew's potato lifting record. I'd say he was the strongest man in the County. I was standing next to him, he was pointing at something. The ball went right in his eye and took the back of his head off. Who is going to look after the farm and all those kids?"

"Why did we meet here and slaughter each other? I killed sixteen-year-old boys today and a lot of old men. You know, Ez, I can't believe what we did. I charged down off this hill with an empty rifle. Did you see Colonel Chamberlain leading us with an empty revolver? What made us do it? I guess the blood being up, and it was the right thing to do. It was also the only thing to do, without giving up the whole ridge. Ezra, the Colonel says we saved the Army of the Potomac. Most of us are gone, but the Colonel says what we did here today will be remembered."

"Jake, do you see that town away off to the right, that's Gettysburg. The 11th Corps retreated through there last evening, running like a hog from slaughter. The whole damn army of the Potomac is up on this ridge now. We are up here to stay. God help Johnny if he tries to push us off. This will be our Fredericksburg, our Marye's Heights.

"How's the pain Jacob?"

"Ez, I'm thirsty as hell, just wet my lips. Don't go down to Plum Run for water, they'll nail you from the Den. It's a real bad gut shot, it hurts. I always feared a gut shot. I know there is nothing you can do for me, just don't let them put me in a wagon. I should be gone by morning. How's your leg, Ezra?"

"I'm not going to let them take it. That leg is going back to Maine attached to my carcass, dead or alive. I wouldn't be worth a damn at home. Big Matthew and I have ran our last race. Could you see me pulling stump or swinging an ax with one shank? Yesterday, I helped carry Josh to the field hospital in back of the Third Corps. He was dead when we got there. You don't want to see what's going on over there or hear that screaming. They got legs piled up like ears of corn right out side the opening of the cutting tent."

"Ezra, look on the far side of that open field. There must be about ten thousand Rebs falling into rank. WOW! GOSH! What in tarnation! All hell is loose! God, their artillery must have opened up with every one of their pieces. They seem to be concentrating on that clump of oaks in our center, that's Hancock's outfit. Oh God, do you see what's happening, they are firing too high, most of their shells are falling into Meade's headquarters, and the hospital, area. Everything is going up, men, horses, tents; what slaughter."

"Jake, they should be able to hear that in Maine, must be the loudest sound ever heard. I have never seen anything like this. This has to be the largest sustained cannonade of the war. They finally stopped, but my ears are still ringing. I think those Rebs on the edge of the field are starting to move out.

"God, look Jacob! They are going to try and cross that field and hit our center. That's almost a mile, they don't have a chance. They are marching into a slaughter pen! They will be cut to pieces. Hancock's Second Corps is waiting for them. They'll have time to pick and choose. Look at all those flags flowing in the wind, how the bayonets reflect the sun, they look magnificent. There is only one man on a horse. Their ranks, arrow straight, no hurry to their step, not a shot or sound from them, only the music of Dixie. They are all going to their death, and by God they know it.

"Our artillery along our whole line, from Culps Hill to here, is pouring it into them. Now they're falling under flanking fire of both our cannon and rifles. We got men in that gully on their left flank, only a hundred yards from them. Each ball is taking out two men. When their ranks break they just close up and keep coming. They are determined. It's Fredericksburg, all over again. I can't believe it. It's murder.

"They have reached the half way mark and have broken into a trot. I can hear that damn yell. I can't believe the bravery of such men. Oh God, each cannon shot takes out a dozen. Their officers are down and still they come. Look at the holes in their ranks. Why don't they go back?

"That looks like their last officer, the one out in front, he has his hat on the point of his sword. They are guiding on him. He's pointing to that little clump of oaks. What a target, can you imagine how many sights he's in? He's down; he must weigh a thousand pounds. I wouldn't want to count the minies in him. Jacob, look they made it to the trees, some of them have climbed over that stone wall where it angles. It's hand to hand! They have captured a piece at the angle. They are starting to break. Why in hell did they do it? My God! Look at that field! Jacob, do you see? ...Jacob? ...JACOB!?"

Greenwich Village Collage

Greenwich Village is that one watering hole that must be seen and tasted by those who wish to know New York. If you're single, hungry for adventure, and a non-conformist, it's worth a year of your life. You will meet fellow pilgrims who appear from every part of the country seeking a sort of Camelot; some find it.

I loved the restaurants, the bars, the sidewalk art shows, antique shops, little theaters, and playing chess in Washington Square. The people from the New School, New York University, Parsons, Cardozo, Forbes, Prentice Hall, Fairchild, Sheed & Ward, Marshall Chess Club, and Asti's restaurant, where all the help sing opera. There are the con games: the handkerchief switch, three card Monty, the supposed "moron," who has just found gold coins on the subway and ask you for advice. The pick-pocket who catches you in the swinging door, or puts ketchup on you when you are going up a staircase and calls out, "You've been shot." While you're ripping your coat off, he walks away with the briefcase you have just put down. The supposedly stolen watch, peeking out of the folded newspaper and the whispered, "How about it, Mac, ten bucks?" Your friendly mugger, who can do a job on you in ten seconds, in broad daylight. I admired them, all but the mugger, he plays too rough. What you see in the Village quite often ain't what you get. If you wish to tour the Village keep one hand on your heart, the other on your wallet and one eye in the back of your head.

Thirty years ago I descended into a "hole" in the ground, smack in the middle of the Village. The "hole" was actually a bank's safe deposit vault where I was employed. To describe the "hole" where I spent a great part of my life, I could compare it to a hermitage. Those who wander down into the "hole" looking for a place to hide their wealth would wonder how I could stand the solitude. Little did they know from whence I came. In my misspent youth I had become addicted to chess and darn near lived in Washington Square Park. I was just a wood pusher who loved the game. As the saying goes, "I don't think I ever beat a well man." I was once taken apart by a sightless man in thirty moves. If the world is a stage, I met my share of fellow performers, and it was quite a show. Over the years, many members of the cast have sat at my desk. .

All I could offer them was my two floppy ears. I did not attempt to untie the knots. I left that to the hundreds of psychotherapists who infested the Village at the time. I found that the common denominator among us all was that we liked to be listened to, and that we needed a lot of loving. Each one of us exists in a different space and time that hides our interdependence. Not blind to our basic oneness, we attempt to reach out to one another.

As the strangers sat at my desk the first thing said would be, "Are they all your kids?" I had a frame on the wall that held small cameo pictures of my adversaries. They then asked me how I managed. I replied that I had never come close. I gave the person, a brief glimpse of life in the trenches and we would commence to bond.

Most people, believe it or not, are human. They would warmly accept me as a fellow member of the walking wounded. Their need to heal and be healed would surface. There was a mystical touching, a willing to trust and risk letting me into their lives. They filled out a brief application that told me enough about their background to pick their locks, permitting me to draw out the highlights of the life of one of God's greatest creations. I loved them all for taking the time to sit and share. I have few gifts but one I always enjoyed was being a good listener.

I showed heartfelt interest in their lives and they repaid me in kind. No one wore a mask at my desk. There was no need not to be honest. I know their love and wisdom made a huge difference in my handling life's problems. Humanity is like a group therapy session that's just not running too smoothly. We really do need a Moderator.

Customers sitting at my desk carried me on voyages of wild adventure, of deep tragedy, the greatest moments in their lives, their dreams of success, how it was to grow up in Spleedunk. They shared their feelings of isolation and loneliness, even of contemplating suicide. Three of my customers told me of their plans and the good listener failed to hear them. I guess I had more hope for them than they did.

Individuals described the part they were playing in the big show, from the Mayor's bagman to Frank Sheed, (we had a mutual love of Augustine), and Malcolm Forbes. I had his Faberge Collection. I would let him look at it once in a while.

There was the resident of the Bowery, an old shaggy bum who held his pants up with a piece of cord. He wore a copper washer for a ring. I was always alarmed that the bank was going to throw him out. He loved to play the horses. When he died, as was the custom, we opened his safe deposit box. He may not have beaten the world, but he beat the horses: three thousand bucks in cash, a winner.

From the psychiatrist who told me she had treated homosexuals in the village for thirty years, and never met a mother who wasn't glad her son was a homosexual.

The practicing child psychiatrist who always mummified her safe deposit box with red masking tape, and constantly accused me of putting things from her kitchen into the box. Outside of that she was as sane as you are, I think. Ninety-nine percent of the time she was perfectly normal. We got along great, but she was always disappointed in me when she found strange things in her box. One time she had a police captain from the local precinct call me up and tell me to knock it off. He did not need an explanation.

There was the psychiatrist who always had a big grin on his face, not a smile. I figured this guy must have solved the problem. I finally asked him, "What's the answer, Doc?"

Not removing the grin, he answered, "Heavy sedation."

The writer, who told me her novel was about to be reviewed in the Daily and Sunday Times the following week. That Friday I picked her book up at the local bookstore, intending to give it a preview reading. I spent a busy weekend with my head in her book. She was a superb writer, a master of the English language. She picked her words, like the Colombians pick their beans. Her phrases were memorable. I constantly paused to admire her style, but the book was god-awful. The meat of the story was the reminiscences of the main character, a dowager. She told of a life born in poverty and dying in immense wealth, at the age of ninety. Her life had been pure self-gratification, without conscience or regret. Adultery, stealing, poisoning her Down's syndrome grandchild, vice after vice, all perfectly justified. The heroine would have made a great spouse for Sammy of "What Makes Sammy Run?" I always thought you enjoyed a book or were bored by it, not so. I was disgusted with it. The parting words of the heroine, "And I have been lied to." She should have been shot. The author's writing skills were acknowledged in both reviews. I doubt if Rembrandt could sell a masterpiece of vomit.

The Fifth Avenue dentist who gave me $3,000 worth of treatment and would only take twenty bucks. He was a Navy dentist who I had served with on Guam. The nicest words I ever heard, "That will be twenty dollars." I was set to drop a bundle. I made it up to him in referrals.

The heart surgeon, with a huge income, told me he couldn't afford his insurance and was going to quit. I grunted with sympathy, as my intestine popped, from carrying his share of the world's wealth.

How it was to tour Russia as a reporter for a top financial magazine. The reporter was actually an editor of the magazine, a chap who, no doubt, was an expert on the world economy. He told me what a joke it was to see a lock factory that had to fulfill its quota by tonnage, meet it by making huge locks. He had toured their factories and couldn't believe what he had seen. Still in a state of shock, he gave me all the details of his trip and then I read it in the magazine. In 1970 he knew the U.S.S.R was doomed.

I asked the late Paul Ford who was starring in "It's Never Too Late," how he remembered his lines. He always spoke as if he was very mixed up. I don't think he ever acted. Paul Ford of the "Bilko Show" and "The Russians Are Coming" was Paul Ford, period. "I don't" he replied, "I know just about what to say. Every night my lines are a little different." He was one humble person.

I met the old New York Times reporter, F.W. Marquand, who covered Buffalo Bill's Wild West Show and knew Cody, and also knew James Barrie, author of "Peter Pan". Imagine talking to someone who knew "Buffalo Bill."

Then there was Jack Rose, the very last of the bare-knuckle fighters. A nice little man, about ninety when I met him. He fought as a bantam. There was always an unbelievable amount of rounds in each of his fights.

In one of the clippings he showed me he was wearing a jewel-studded belt. He was a winner. He was a cream puff. What a simple guy! He was huggable. I couldn't picture him hurting anyone.

There was also the guy who had a swimming pool in his mansion, next to his bed, my fondest dream. Each morning he jumped out of bed into his pool. One of the finest men I have ever met, yet when he told me of his baggage I knew I would never have the courage to jump into his pool. Life is very fair. It's unfair to everyone.

How would you like to be owner of one of worlds top publishing houses, and give each of your nephews and nieces a million dollars on their twenty-first birthday. Don't forget to take his special daughter with you. She is the woman standing in the corner facing the wall. The world is very fair.

The member of the John Birch Society who had about fifty pounds of South African krugerrands in his box and was waiting for the U.S. to collapse; "any day."

The artist who gave me one of his paintings and then a month later jokingly accused me of hanging it under my bed. I told him, " Stay out of my bedroom."

The people who become captives of their wealth. Sometimes I actually thought the vault would pulsate. There were so many hearts locked in it. People would call me to ask me to check if their box was locked.

That reminds me of the time I asked a multi-millionaire friend, how it was to be rich. He looked me straight in the eye and said, " I'm not rich. I'll tell you who's rich. You should meet the guy whose yacht is tied up next to mine down at Palm Beach. What a yacht!" That's when I learned we are all rich, and we are all poor, depending in which direction you're looking.

The countless clothing magnates who lived near the bank on Fifth Avenue who always died twenty years too soon. A bunch of regular guys from the old neighborhood.

The countless widows of the countless magnates who died twenty years too soon. The countless sons of the countless magnates who had never taken over their father's business, instead, beat it out to California. One old friend worked all his life to build a thriving clothing store. Two months after his death his son closed the store and sold the building for eight million dollars. I asked his son, whom I knew since he was a kid, how it was to have eight million bucks. He said it wasn't all that good. He lost all his old friends. When out dining with his buddies, if he picked up the check, he made them look bad, if they paid, he was cheap.

The thousands of young actors and actresses who came into the Village to give New York a whack. The one lesson they had to learn, "If you don't think you're better than Tom Hanks or Meryl Streep go home." You have to have one heck of an ego to succeed in the theater. The competition eats all but the tigers. It's not really a "Wonderful Town." I met a few who made it, but not many.

The poor soul, who survived Belsen, needed no tattoo. His eyes and skull-like face told it all. He said when he went into the camp; he was a devout Jew. Now he firmly believed that Moses met no one and heard nothing on top of that mountain. Top that for tragedy. He never really survived. That man was dead. He was a ghost haunting the living. I wish I had never met him. I never asked him for his story. Just to look at him made me nauseous with guilt. That painful reflex action gave me quite an insight into who is our brother's keeper.

The millions of dollars of diamond jewelry shown to me that could not be worn because of the crime in our society and not sold because, "My late husband gave it to me;" actually worthless to the owner.

The very distinguished gentleman, with Homburg and velvet collared coat, who only walked backwards. What a strange, horrible illness. Ask your father "what's a Homburg?"

Learning never to ask how the wife is, if you hadn't seen her for a while. Divorce was a popular past time in the Village.

The lady who removed every stitch of her clothes, down to the buff, sans shoes or stockings, on the bank floor. She had been told that she lacked sufficient I.D. for the bank to cash her check. "How's this for I.D.?" The rest of the customers completely ignored her (the subway syndrome). I had come up on the bank floor to make a deposit. You could hear that pin drop. A customer whispered to me. "Do you think she has a gun?" I looked her over carefully and replied, "I doubt it." The cool Officer In Charge walked up and asked, "What seems to be the problem?" The greatest understatement I ever heard. You bet we cashed her check.

The Admiral, classmate and friend of Rickover, who headed a destroyer flotilla, was now a lawyer. His destroyers ran cover for our convoy when the outfit was on its way to Iwo. He had served on some of the same ships my father was stationed on. I became a close friend of his father who was a very wise old rabbi. I dined with the rabbi at his home, a very kind soul. The whole family was a class act.

The Koreans own all the dry cleaning stores in New York City. Great money if you want to put the time in. One young Korean told me he had to go to Boston in order to locate a store that was for sale. This young man was what America is all about; both he and his wife, upon getting out of Parsons, put their careers as commercial artists on hold. They managed at one time or another to obtain a Laundromat, a restaurant and now they were seeking a dry cleaning business. Shortly after his return from Boston he told me his only child crawled out the window of his twelve-story apartment on Sixth Ave. Sometimes it just doesn't pay to make friends.

The Korean girls, who worked the massage parlor around the corner from the bank, all had Irish last names and married GIs to get over here. They made a ton of money the hard way, five hundred to a thousand a day, tax-free. The average girl worked a year, made a large grubstake, then would take off to open a 7-11 out west somewhere. They all looked like sweet young things, living on the razor edge, in very rough company. The courts finally shut them down. I heard their language, when testifying, was so innocently gross, the judge had to clear the court.

The voice coach, who always invited me to observe his class of aspiring students on graduation night. He would book a club in the Village so they could perform live. I think his students always thought I was on a talent search. I felt a little guilty when some of his students would fawn over me. I thought his singers were great, but some of his comedians were hilariously lousy. Talk about chutzpah. He was a good coach, but he wouldn't take the responsibility for their material. He himself was a natural comedian and I enjoyed his company, a good friend for many years.

God, did I know widows; some never cry, and some never stop. With their husband gone, most wives had no idea how to handle their finances. As time passed they lost touch with reality. It was painful to see the Fifth Avenue dowager facing Alzheimer's alone.

I'll never forget the poor shrew that tortured her husband constantly, a hell of a nice guy. He had five chairs in his dental office and left her a fortune. He worked himself to death. Upon his death she never stopped recalling, "The man was a saint". The poor woman for years was constantly in tears. They are from further out then Venus.

Quite often these women forgot to eat, or pay any of their utilities. I kept a lot of telephones ringing and lights on. Sometimes I actually opened their pocketbooks to see if they had enough money to buy food, or I took money out of their accounts and paid the old bills that they carried, and gave them enough money for the week. They thought they were destitute because their pocketbook was empty, when in actuality they were extremely well off. They would constantly forget that they had accounts with us. The wife of the dentist dressed in rags and always thought she was broke. I went through their safe deposit boxes hunting coupon bearing bonds that sometimes had not been clipped in years. They would be so grateful when I found several thousand dollars of their own money. They wanted me to take half of it, but I never did. It was sad. It was so easy for these women to fall through the cracks. Those, whose children had long ago moved to California and called Mom once in awhile. Then there were the childless, or the poor wretches who had planned their own lonely demise. They were prey to the unscrupulous. When a relative eventually showed up, I could only cross my fingers and hope for the best. The best long-term investment is still children, but there are no sure things.

The people upstairs must have suspected what I was doing, but I think they preferred not to believe it, so "unbankish". "Money and Banking" and "The Mathematics of Finance" were not my strong suits. I blew both of them in college. Thank God, I majored in Philosophy, I never regretted it. To me the bank was always a vapor, an illusion. I could never relate to it. Don't misunderstand me I was always loyal to my employer, but in my fashion. They came out far ahead.

I enjoyed the close relationship I maintained with my customers, and naturally I paid a price. A tear accompanied every laugh I shared with them.

I had a lot of gay friends who were caught in that sudden chilling wind that came from nowhere. I remembered my mother had often mentioned the horror she had witnessed during the influenza epidemic of 1918. She had worked as a maid in a doctor's office in New York City. The doctor would come home and empty his pockets of all his money, and she would put it in a basket to be placed out on a windowsill. The flu was taking whole families. AIDS was reaping only the young men, but oh so thoroughly. Outside of San Francisco, there are probably more gays in the Village, per square foot then any other place in our country. The gays who lived in the Village were only in the closet if they worked in an up or downtown office. Most of the gays I knew were either in the theater or the fashion industry. A great bunch, but I did feel a definite gap between us. Their world was gay but I thought I sensed a bitterness they felt toward the establishment, a hidden anger. There was an invisible line drawn, or maybe a fence that kept our worlds apart. They had more than their share of talent and it seemed, good looks. They also had a sharp and caustic wit, but I also felt they were extremely lonely.

It was sad seeing the effeminate gay trying to built up his immune system by going on steroids, taking up bodybuilding, which was completely out of character. I watched as so many of them slowly started to fail, fade and die. It was so damn certain. Every gay was terror-stricken. The past could not be undone. When the young men died, I met their grieving families, who came to the Village from all over the country. They would go down to the vault to empty the safe deposit box. It doesn't get much sadder. As I sit here I can conjure up a sea of faces of dead friends. They all took a part of me with them. Time lock set. Vault door closed, I sit in a bar across the street from the Bank, downing a Manhattan. I have come to the conclusion that the only thing of real value in my vault were the people who came into it.

Who Said Solid Rock?

Minetta Stream ran quietly in the substratum beneath my feet. I first became aware of the stream when I was poking through book-shelves in the cellar of the old Dauber and Pine bookstore (long gone) across the street from my bank. It was a bookstore that actual-ly belonged in London around 1850. When it closed my heart broke. The proprietors were two ancient gnomes, about as old as you can get. The last of their kind, the keepers of the ancient books.

I always enjoyed exploring the lower depths of the store during my lunch hour. On one occasion while in their cellar, wondering up and down the dark aisles, pulling long light strings off and on, I found myself for the first time in a dark corner that reeked with foul dampness. I had a hard time breathing this almost liquid air.

After pulling on a long string that lit a bare bulb dangling from the high ceiling, I noticed in the faint light, that the books that were on the shelves against the wall, were covered with a heavy coat of what resembled moss more than mildew.

I removed a book to check the damage to the pages. Luckily the books were packed so tightly; the damage to the pages was insignifi-cant. The title of the book I had randomly picked startled me, Acts & Laws of the Massachusetts Bay Colony. The book was published in 1692. Thinking the book to be of some interest and value, I approached one of the old gentlemen, either Dauber or Pine, never could get their names straight. Both were cute little bald fat guys. I believe it was Mr. Pine. He was wearing one of those green eyeshades that the old scriptors used. His glasses were vintage Ben Franklin. He was seated at an old beat-up desk in the center of the maze of shelves. He gave the book but a brief glance and quoted a ten-dollar price. When I asked for the cause of the extreme dampness in that part of the cellar, he explained that an underground stream called Minetta, ran beneath the wall and on occasion its level would rise and the dampness seeped through the walls.

I was always led to believe the NY was build on solid rock. Was there a stream under the Twin Towers? Not wanting to pass up such a strange find, I hastened back across the street to my bank and cleaned out my account. In a brief moment, with the ten dollars clutched in my hand, I was back in D&P's cellar closing the sale. That afternoon I hastened my moss-coated friend to the rare book section of the New York Public Library and inquired if they had a copy of "Acts & Laws of the Massachusetts Bay Colony". After a short wait the clerk returned, carrying a book on a pillow. He placed the book still resting on the pillow, on a table for my perusal.

He was rather surprised when I reached into my diaper bag, that served as my bookbag, (before the time of backpacks) and showed him my copy. Asking the value of it, he gave me a list of rare-book dealers that would buy the book. He said the book was worth approx-imately about $600 and much more if it was refurbished. I was natu-rally surprised to see Dauber and Pine were on the list. I felt rather guilty about a sale. I could never sell it, and surely a waste to keep it in my own library. I read my copy without a pillow and then donated it to the Jesuits. There were two items mentioned in the book that stuck in my mind. One was the law that any woman caught in adul-tery would be forced to wear the scarlet letter "A" on her breast. The second was that a bounty of two pounds would be paid for any Indian's scalp, who was over the age of 12. It made me think that we might have taught the "savage" the art of scalping. It also mentioned that Jesuits were not "persona grata" in the Massachusetts Bay Colony.

The second time I ran into the Minetta Stream was when I noticed that one of the walls of my "hole" was so damp that it was deteriorating. I could hear excavation on the other side and I decid-ed to investigate.

Down in the adjoining bowel of the building next door I found a construction worker, who told me, while sinking a shaft for a new ele-vator, fresh water kept filling up the hole. They were puzzled and thought they had cracked a water main. They were stashing yards of wet sand along our common wall, causing seepage into my domain. I mentioned Minetta stream and how contrary to popular belief, Manhattan is not built on solid rock, "A River Runs Through It", or words to that effect.

Square One

I remember as a child, when I would lie in bed in the pitch dark, mystified by the thinking brain resting on the pillow. It pulsed with life. I was it, but who and what was it. I was told I was a child of God, and when I died I would be with him. That answer sufficed for the hereafter, but who was this child of God living on this planet.

It just boggled my mind. I knew I was alive, but what was I? I existed, but why? I knew nothing of myself. I would feel like a piece of driftwood that just showed up in the current. What am I doing here? I am part of this world and yet I am separate. Who am I?

Now I'm no longer a child, but deep in my seventies. I think back on how I was stymied as a child, trying to figure out the great mystery of me. Now I laugh at the simplicity of the answer. I realize now why I was boggled.

The answer can only come when one understands that life is like a voyage and our destination remains a secret to ourselves. Only when the voyager makes his landfall can he look back at his wake and understand who and what he is. When he looks back he will see nothing. Nothing is ever left in the wake. There is no past. The now of one moment ago is as real as the now of seventy years ago. Nothing has been lost. Each individuals passage is unique, a series of memory links.

The who, and what I am is the summation of the nows. Time is only a man made filing cabinet. Let me give you an example. I stand outside the church, where I have just witnessed my daughter's wedding. My heart burst with emotion as I recall the event. Almost instantaneously I recall holding her in my arms on the day of her birth. Which thought is the most real, the moment of her wedding or the moment of her birth?

Both those memories are me. The marriage memory has added to my being. What I actually am at any given moment is the composite of all my memories. I am memory.

My most pleasurable moments our spent sitting under the old oak tree at the edge of the lake. Here is where I live it all over again, always my favorite thinking spot. I close my eyes and it all comes rushing back: the games of stickball, those three sewer-shots; playing ringa-leaveo, thinking your lungs will explode as you ran; Gad, what ever happened to marbles; those high school days, I wonder what ever happened to Helen, forever sixteen; I remember the guys in Charlie Company- their faces still so clear; my first car, the 28 Studebaker (now there was a wreck); dancing at Happy's Yacht Club the night I proposed to Dot; seven kids, fifteen grandchildren and a house with love and laughter pouring out doors and windows. All I had to do was concentrate and ancient tears and smiles would once more appear on this face, weathered by the years.

"Your husband has Alzheimer disease. His MRI shows the white matter of his brain has greatly deteriorated. This condition is expressed in severe memory loss. A memory loss of such severity leaves the mind completely blank. What primarily distinguishes us from one another and is the source of the "self" is our memory. Your husband is no longer in touch with reality. His brain cell deterioration has progressed to such a point he can only live his life as he lived it as an infant, possibly a one year old. All his answers have been destroyed your husband is only left with questions."

Who are these people? Why am I here? What am I supposed to do? Why doesn't my Mother come? Who is this strange person who cleans me and dresses me? I don't know her. What does she mean that we have been married for fifty years?

Objects are placed in front of me and I'm told to eat my food. What is eat? What is food? I'm told to use my knife and fork. What is use? What is knife? What is fork? I lie in my bed in the pitch dark, mystified by my thinking brain resting on my pillow. Who am I? Why am I here? I want my Mother.

The Man With The Shovel

It was two days before Christmas. Dot left for work at her usual time, 7:10 AM.. I lay in bed for ten minutes before I entered my morning shower. Following my usual routine, I had twenty minutes before I left the house for church. I jumped into the shower at 7:20. I would normally shower for ten minutes, get dressed and be on my way by 7:50, but this morning called for a little more hustle. The weather report stated that we had received two inches of snow during the night and we could expect another six before in ended. While showering, I pleasantly visualized our town having a white Christmas. I suddenly realized what was about to happen. "Oh, God," I cried out to heaven, "I hope I'm not too late."

I jumped from my shower without touching a towel, threw on a pair of pants and a sweatshirt. Slipped my wet feet into my slippers and catapulted down the stairs. I flung open the door. Too late, five to ten minutes at the most. This I could deduce by the markings in the snow. My wife had left the house at 7:10 and her footprints were not as fresh as those left by the thief. It was now only 7:25.

I had left my new shovel in the vestibule, but last night Dot had mistakenly thought it best to place it out on the porch. I was attached to this shovel. It was a beauty; not one of those tinny snow-shovels, where the edges always bend on you. Mine was one of those large coal shovels. The beauty of it was that the bucket of the shovel was made of a bright red, stout plastic and was extremely light.

I normally would have jumped back into the warm house, cursing fate, regretfully writing off the shovel, but I remembered I had purchased the last shovel in our local store. Those footprints were just too fresh to ignore. I had to act immediately. I knew the snow and the wind would soon hide this foul deed. If I were to get my man there would be no time to hitch the dogs and put on my furs. The game was afoot.

I flew off the porch in hot pursuit, despite my leaving the shower soaking wet only a minute before. I had no choice; the blood was up. As I dogged my quarry, I closely studied the fresh prints. Calling upon my deductive powers once more, my mind soon produced a clear picture of the culprit. By his small shallow print he could not weigh more than 140 pounds and probably under five feet. It was also obvious he was wearing worn sneakers, which would only denote a man of poor circumstance. The act itself, stealing in broad daylight and knowing he would leave tracks, betrayed him as a desperate man.

His was the only track and headed off in the opposite direction than my wife. I planned on a quick encounter with the scoundrel, but it was not to be. The clearness of the track did not indicate that he was running, yet after a chase that led me up a steep hill and down several blocks, and around corners, he was still nowhere in sight. I could see that he was attempting to conceal his trail by walking on the grass that bordered the sidewalk. In spite of the cake of frost on my wet head and the wind blown snow keeping my eyes to slits, I was actually enjoying the game. I guess there is a little cat in all of us.

Finally I spotted my target a half a block away, a red spot on the shoulder of a small figure. The cat was about to spring. As I hurried my pursuit, my conscience escaped from its dungeon, forcing me to concede to a painful truth. I was chasing today's "Jean Valjean." I was on the trail of a Guat.

I was pursuing a shovel that would remove snow from a few blocks of my cement walk. My quarry was escaping with a precious tool that would sustain his wife and children during his months of unemployment. I stopped in my tracks. I felt a strong need to return to my shower to cleanse myself.

Hoping there was a little Finn in me, I reentered the hot shower to stave off the risk of pneumonia. As the sweltering water beat upon my shivering body, the picture that the track revealed was all too clear. He was from Guatemala, small of statue, dark eyes, Indian features and jet-black hair. He had been smuggled into our country, leaving his family in their poverty stricken village. I knew him well.

He lived in a small slum apartment in town with probably seven to ten other countrymen, each paying twenty dollars a week to an unscrupulous landlord. My picture of the thief fit any one of the hundreds of illegal Guatemalans that dwelled among us. To me they really do look alike. Most of these men are between the age of seventeen and thirty. There are no Guatemalan women here.

At dawn, during the course of the summer, every corner on the main drag has a swarm of Guats shaping up. Pickup trucks owned by small contractors, usually in the landscape or building business, pick up what wee people they need for a days labor. They are paid next to nothing.

It is an embarrassment to pass a Guat on the street. As you approach him, he will give you much more room then you deserve. He will hang his head attempting to avoid any eye contact and any sort of confrontation. It brings to mind the Deep South during the height of segregation.

Compared to their small statue, we must appear to them as giants. In about thirty years, when the Guats have become the community and we have fled, they will tell their grandchildren about us. "There were giants in those days."

They are not welcome in town and are uniformly disliked for being illegal, small, poor, and Indian. I don't like them because they are small, poor and Indian; I don't mind them being illegal. I remember my father jumped ship in order to plant the Kias root. On second thought, he was rather small, broke, and a dirty Mick.

You can always spot the apartments the Guats live in, by noticing how the windows are wide open and the curtains are tied in a knot. This is done during the stifling summer months, so as not to obstruct the flow of air in their sweatboxes. God knows what kind of heat they received in the winter.

As I had mentioned, the main reason they had come to our town and accepted almost slave-like conditions was to send money home to their poverty-stricken families. Before they can do this, the Guats have to amass some cash for a bicycle. In no way can they afford public transportation. You can tell who is a new arrival in town; the poor guy wobbles down the street struggling to master his new,"old," bike. Quite often they have to pedal tremendous distances to and from their job.

Occasionally the Department of Immigration will sweep into town and unsuccessfully attempt to round them up. While this is going on, the town has the appearance that we are indulging in a giant game of "manhunt." Guats are barreling out of doors and windows, running in all directions, pursued by the agents.

Being illegal, they are at the mercy of any individual who has a mean streak in him, and that takes in a lot of us. The young hoods in town mug them at their leisure, taking what little money they have and even their precious cigarettes. They know they can't go to the police. One of our police sergeants was witless enough to be quoted in the paper: "The Police Department is not responsible for their protection." Can you believe that?

On the way home from work on payday, they try to travel in pairs. At nightfall, you will very seldom see a Guat walking alone. One was found murdered two days before the last town election. The town kept a lid on the event, only briefly stating that an unidentified man was found dead in an empty lot. After the election, it was reported that he had died from several stab wounds and that his countrymen had identified him the night of the murder.

The flow of the Guats into our town has not ebbed. More and more are coming in each year. You don't notice them arriving; they just seem to pop out of the ground. There must be an Underground Railroad station in our midst.

Due to their dependence upon seasonal employment, winter brings on desperate times. Condemned to live in the shadows, they cannot appeal for public aid. Our parish now has a Spanish speaking priest who can offer them a Sunday Mass. The parish helps as best it can.

As I dried myself I realized that the morning chase could have ended in a very painful incident. I thank God he kept us apart. What was one man's snow, was another man's manna.

You Can Take It With You

I sat on the sand watching the breakers beat upon the beach. I found it hard to believe that I had been on Maura for five years. The early morning surf fishing finished, I gathered up my gear and ambled up to my villa on the hill. By my appearance, I could be taken for a native islander. The part of my body that was not covered by my sarong was brown as a coffee bean. My long, white hair, partially covered by a red bandanna, was tied in a knot.

On deciding to become a permanent resident on the island, I purchased a large tract of beach property and had a villa erected on the hill overlooking a lagoon on one side, and the endless Pacific on the other. I had brought the blueprints of my new home with me, all part of my retirement plan. I imported the workers and material from Kyushu for its construction. It cost a fortune, but as my father always said, "If you got it, spend it" and I did have it. It had all the comforts one would want and yet not ostentatious. I made sure it wasn't the San Simeon of Maura.

I had only been seated on my verandah for a moment when Gabriela, my beautiful native companion, approached with my morning libation, rye and vermouth. A drink named after another island that would never again feel my footfall.

We silently held hands for a moment as we shared the sea breeze. Gabriela was tall and graceful, with long black hair draped over her shapely mahogany form. I had never seen such perfect teeth; their whiteness brought out the stark black of her eyes. I never tired admiring her beauty. She was my true treasure; my money was only a tool.

Without speaking, she departed back into the villa. I sipped on my drink looking out at, and yet not seeing, my Pacific bulwark. I thought how marvelous it was that we should meet. Gabriela had become, as they say, the very beat of my heart. Our villas were the only two on the hill. What started out as being good neighbors grew into a powerful love relationship. Our strange encounter came about one evening while I stood on my verandah gazing at the moon reflecting off the ocean. I was suddenly captivated by the sound of a haunting violin drifting through the night air. It was Mendelssohn's Allegro Molto Appassionato, which had always held me spellbound. The music was emanating from the home of my only neighbor on the hill. I knew a woman occupied the villa, but I had never seen her. I followed the sound of the music as if in a daze. I found myself standing in her garden, entranced by her virtuosity.

After hearing the last note, I could not resist going to her door and introducing myself. The occupant came to the door with the instrument still in hand. Her beauty was only excelled by her music. I thanked her for the most ecstatic rendition of the Appassionato that I had ever heard. She smiled graciously, accepting my compliments, and saying that she thought it was time we met. Had she been calling me?

It was the beginning of a relationship that I could only compare to the gift of Eve to Adam. The highlight of our time together was when this gorgeous woman joined me on my verandah each evening to play for me. With the haunting sound of a beguine filling the night air, the palms swaying beneath the moon, I would be caught up in a reverie of years long past.

The trinket about her neck sparkled in the bright moonlight. The Gates necklace was shown at it's best when worn by a beautiful woman, not hidden away in a vault. I had presented it to Gabriela with the understanding that she would never wear it off the hill. I told her I still hadn't had it insured and a thing of such beauty would only cause envy and jealousy among our beloved friends. She had no idea of its history or value.

Gabriela was a descendent of Captain Nathaniel Savory, a whaler from New Bedford, who had settled on Maura in 1830. She was educated in Japan and studied music in Australia. While there she became an accomplished violinist. During a musical tour in Australia, she met and married a physician and bore him two children. Her husband was killed during the war while serving in New Guinea. Never recovering from this loss, she returned to Maura alone after raising her children. Though she was in great demand to tour the continent, she preferred seclusion on the island. It was a tragic loss to the music world.

We were extremely close, but I never revealed to Gabriela my past background or true identity. Bill Kias had ceased to exist. I had mailed my son a letter on the last day on the job, telling him how I would always treasure our past relationship and would never forget him. I knew my boy was involved with his own family and would stand the pain of my loss.

There was no doubt in my mind, that the careful effort and length of time I had expended to be here, had been a small price to pay for the rapture I now enjoyed.

*　　　*　　　*

"Mr. Shaw, sir. This is Jim Bates. I'm down in the vault. I'm the new Vault Manager."

"Yes, Jim, how can I help you?"

"Well sir, my very first customer, a Mrs. Ziner, tells me the box that I removed from her safe is not hers. She is mad as hell! Could you come down here? What do I do? I've got four customers waiting!"

Shaw thought that old guy Kias must have taken care of two customers at the same time, which is a no-no. He returned the two boxes into the vault in one trip, placing them in the wrong safes. It was the only possible way he could place the tins in the wrong safes.

"Stay cool, Jim, I'm on my way. Take care of the other customers. Place Mrs. Ziner in one of your conference rooms."

As Shaw headed downstairs to the vault, he thought that old Kias, who had retired Friday, should have gotten out much earlier. You can't spend twenty years in a vault without losing it.

He hadn't met Jim yet. He knew he was fresh out of Yale and had just started the Bank's Officers Training Program. He was going to work as a Vault Manager for a two-month stint, part of the course, and then move to back office and up the line.

Shaw found it hard to believe what Jim had reported about the switch. It just couldn't happen. Kias had written the Safe Deposit Manual. He taught classes at the training center covering every aspect of the security required for an efficient, safe deposit facility.

It was an extremely controlled environment that called for a thorough yearly audit. Every facet of gaining access and locking a safe deposit box had been written in cement for at least a hundred years. In today's crime ridden society, the safe deposit facility is the last bastion for the protection of an individual's valuables.

The bank, assuming the responsibility for the customer's wealth, takes every possible measure to safeguard it. The customer, when renting the box, is informed that he is receiving the only two keys to his safe. These keys are presented to him in a sealed envelope that have a serial number and a safe number. The customer signs the envelope, verifying that the envelope was given to him sealed. The metal seal could not be broken. The only way to open the envelope was to cut it open with a scissors.

When a safe is surrendered, the keys are to be immediately placed in the slot of a safe to which the Vault Manager does not have access. The Lock Change Company randomly switches the locks from the surrendered boxes upon removing these keys from the safe. The keys are then placed in the sealed key envelopes and the safes re-rented.

The safe contains a tin box into which the customer places his valuables. At each access, he is directed to a small room where he has access to his tin in private. He is told to always keep the tin in full view while it is being removed, carried, and placed back in his safe.

Shaw laughed to himself; the kid certainly sounded shaken. I'll just call up the other customer and soft-soap him to come in with his key. That should do it. His name must be in the tin box. I just hope he isn't a bastard. Shaw felt beat; it's always a pain in the neck to come in after a three-day holiday.

As Shaw approached the vault gate he saw a young man standing behind a desk, surrounded by four extremely irate customers. The guy behind the desk, with his mouth open and white as a sheet, had to be the new man.

As Jim approached the gate to give Shaw access he whispered, "God help us!"

"I gave access to three more customers. They all maintain I have given them the wrong tin. What the hell happened? What am I supposed to say? What do I do with the tins? Mr. Shaw, are we permitted to give out addresses? A Mr. Ortez wants to know Mr. Kias' home address."

Shaw thought, "God, not Mr. Ortez." He was jokingly known as Mr. Coffee in the Branch. He was supposed to have a large "plantation" outside of Cali in Columbia, one tough hombre.

Kias, that son-of-a-bitch, had that bastard switched all the boxes? How the hell did he do it?

Shaw, ignoring the now berserk customers, walked past the desk into the conference room, where he found Mrs. Ziner sitting at a table with someone else's coffer. There was only one way to play it, absolute calm, without a sign of panic.

"We have a little problem here. Lets me just see who owns this box. I'll have him hop over here and you will soon have your box."

Opening it, he quickly managed to identify the owner, a John Cody. Thank God, Shaw knew him.

"John, this is Jack Shaw at the Bank. How are you doing? Great...Listen, could you come over to the Branch for a moment? Come down to the vault. We just want to correct a slight error, and remember to bring your key. Yes, as quickly as possible. Thanks, John."

They waited quietly; Shaw didn't dare go out to Jim's desk where there seemed to be a crowd gathering. Shaw overheard the word "kill" being repeated.

Cody finally showed. He was quite amenable and could understand how Kias, as an old timer in a hurry, could make that error. Cody was an all right guy, thank God. But even at midnight it can get darker. Opening Cody's box it was discovered that a third hand was being dealt. The tin in Cody's safe did not belong to Mrs. Ziner, but to the L.O.L. Abortion Clinic. Mrs. Ziner's box was still missing.

It suddenly hit Shaw, that bastard not only switched the boxes but he did it randomly. How the hell did he do it right in front of their eyes? Kias is the only person who knows where the boxes are. He must have been in every box. What the hell is Head Office going to think of this? One thing for sure, my butt is going to be nailed to the vault door. Before this is over that door is going to be covered with butt. What did Kias know that we didn't? God, help us! What will the newspapers do with this? Our credibility will be destroyed. We had signed contracts with our customers guaranteeing them the safety and confidentiality of the contents of their safes. There won't be an unemployed lawyer for the next ten years.

It was a common belief in the Branch that there was more cash in the customer's safe deposit boxes, than we had in our own safes. It was the largest Branch in New York. The customers, many of them on the Forbes 500 list, were spread all over the globe. The total value of the contents of the safes could only be estimated. The total was sure to run into a multi-million figure.

Shaw thought of a horrible scenario. Harry the Tout opens Von Camps tin in the private room and finds it stuffed with gold kruger-rands. Harry gives the empty box back to Jim, signs a surrender and disappears a winner. A day later Von Camp opens what he thinks is his tin only to find a priceless collection of snuff bottles. All these boxes will have to be sealed and then inventoried. Here was a cata-strophic dilemma. They could only be opened with the permission of the Lessee. How could a customer authorize the opening of a box that did not contain his tin? How would the absent customer feel about their boxes being in the bank's possession without their per-mission? How many boxes belonged to Pandora?

Shaw's mind boggled. Kias must have been planning this for years. There was only one question answered.

"Why do you keep turning down promotion?"

How much did he take? How did he get it out? Why did he ran-domly switch the boxes? Where in the world is Kias? Shaw suddenly remembered Kias' (Pronounced "Chaos") parting words at his retire-ment dinner, "Who said you can't take it with you?"

Where in the world was Kias?

*   *   *

I was on Maura, in the Central Pacific with twenty million in cash, the culmination of my retirement plan.

You say how could he steal that amount?

Planning my boy, planning. Once the plan was conceived it was a piece of strawberry short cake.

The Gotham Safe Deposit Company, whose vaults were situated beneath the branches of the Gotham Bank, had always been a sepa-rate company in order to limit the bank's liability. The bank changed its policy shortly after I was employed. They dissolved the Gotham Safe Deposit Company making each branch responsible for it's own safe deposit facility.

I waited in vain for the creation of a new safe deposit administration to oversee our vaults. It never happened. The bank had not shot itself in the foot, it had cut its own throat. They say every man has his price but this was going to be one heck of an overpayment. My retirement plan first occurred to me when I realized that there was no longer anyone watching the store. The store being one of the largest safe deposit vaults in Gotham City.

The millions in the vault were up for grabs. All that was needed was patience and the conception of a foolproof take-and-keep plan. I knew that Diogenes would be the only person not looking for me.

I first became aware of this strange situation after I received numerous telephone calls on questions concerning safe deposit policy, procedure and accounting practices. I then realized, that by attrition and my long experience, I was becoming known throughout the Bank as the safe deposit authority. When I was stumped for an answer, there was nobody for me to call. I had become God by default.

We were a ship without a rudder, sailing on the sea of Limbo. As far as procedure to be followed, there was no wrong way. The situation was incredible. Our very tight auditing department had ceased to be. The Safe Deposit Manager, being the only person in the branch who knew how to audit the department's keys and locks, became the safe deposit auditor. This was a very unbankish procedure. What hath the Bank wrought?

My spouse had recently passed away. My boy Bill, an F.B.I. Agent, had recently married and had settled on the coast. There was nothing stopping me from going for the gold ring. All the chess pieces were in place. There would be an opening, middle, and an end game. Possibly I had spent too much time in the vault, but I could not turn down the challenge. I was finally answering that haunting call to return to Maura.

I was originally introduced to Maura in 1945, at the close of the war, while serving with a small Marine detachment. Its beauty and isolation immediately struck me. There was no island comparable to it in the Pacific. It had the entire splendor and solitude of the mythical Bali Ha'i. While serving there, I disappeared from my outfit for a week, spending the time as Adam wandering through the Garden of Eden. I had seen enough of hell to know that this was where man was meant to live. My hiatus cost me five days in the brig on piss and punk... well worth it. For twenty years after leaving the island, I never gave up my dream of returning to Paradise.

I would feel no guilt. I had always thought of the bank as a heart-less machine, not a person. The sleeping giant had no idea the game was afoot. The thing had malfunctioned; it could no longer protect its hoard. I would look at it as a financial coup. The system would be held culpable. Jack Shaw was not responsible for the system. He would escape with his hair.

My opening gambit was to gain control of the surrendered safe deposit keys. The fact that the lock-change mechanics switched the locks on surrendered safes, and resealed the keys, was not a problem. I could duplicate the surrendered key and place a matching mark on the back of the lock before I let the key out of my control. This was basically a simple operation. It would take time, but each key could be worth a fortune.

It was easy enough to purchase a key making machine and a supply of key blanks. I was in no hurry. I had all the time in the world. Each night, at home, I duplicated the keys that were surren-dered that day. I then placed the new keys on a concealed pegboard in my basement. When I returned to the job the following day, I placed the customers' keys in the slotted safe belonging to the lock-change mechanics.

I glanced at my mark on the back of the lock when opening a box as a new rental. I noted the box number in my journal, next to the corresponding key. In a fashion, I was slowly moving the largest safe deposit vault in Gotham City into my home.

As the years passed I managed to hang a key on every peg. While the keys were accumulating I carefully planned my flight to Maura. During my leisure time I perused each box, keeping a record of the blocks of stored cash. Oh, the jewelry that people have! But I was only in search of cash. I must admit that my knees buckled when I gazed upon the famous Gates necklace. Forty of the world's most perfect diamonds on one strand. I read it had been appraised at fifteen mil-lion dollars. Should I? I had no intention of taking anything but cash. I would take it, but of course I would never sell it.

I must say I did come across other interesting items such as nar-cotics, guns, and a occasional bottle of whiskey that would add zest to the customer's lunch hour and help him finish his day. In one box I found an ax, covered with dry blood, along with a newspaper clipping mentioning a decapitated Mafia Don. I switched this box with that of a police lieutenant's.

I was quite sure the millions in cash that I had carefully selected from the safes were other people's ill-gotten gains. There was no reason for these large amounts of cash being kept in the vault and not drawing interest. You might say I was going to separate the wheat from the chaff. I had always followed the bank's policy of explaining to the customers when they rented a box that the bank was not responsible for cash. Of course, I knew that a lot of bad guys, including Mr. Coffee's minions would never stop searching for me. It was obvious Mr. Coffee had a laundry problem. The contents of both his boxes were well over two million.

The Mayor's chauffeur, apparently his bagman, was the keeper of a stash of at least a million. He would be no problem. I doubted the chauffeur would ever honk his horn. That was going to be our little secret. I had become a confidant of the Mayor.

My conscience was clear; I had no doubt caused a great deal of confusion, but no lasting damage to any innocent parties. The random switching of the boxes was only a temporary insurance ploy, to be used as a trade-off if my plan had failed and I was forced to barter for a light sentence.

I left a letter in my desk stating that, if I had successfully eluded my pursuers for a month's time, I would provide the bank with my journal designating the location of each tin. Everything going as planned, I lived up to my letter without revealing my whereabouts.

As far as the States were concerned, there was no evidence that Bill Kias had left the country. The FBI had provided Bill Montesque with his name and all his necessary papers, including his passport. My son had used the same documents years before while working undercover for the Bureau. Before the documents were returned, I had managed to duplicate the complete dossier on "the man who never was." I had breathed life into the FBI myth. It would never occur to them that Montesque was alive and a very rich man.

According to the FBI background cover, Montesque had been a design engineer for Lockheed, residing in California. I moved his mailing address to a post office box in Gotham City. I subscribed to several Aerospace journals using Montesque's post office box. He was continually receiving invitations to attend all sorts of aerospace roundtables and lectures in Washington. It seemed that the Bureau had made him a respected associate in his field. It is easier to kill a man then to get him off a mailing list. In fact, up to the time I retired, Montesque appeared to be growing in stature. His silence must have been his strong point. According to Montesque's last change of address, he was now retired and residing on the island of Maura in the Central Pacific. I had managed to hoist the Bureau on their own lie.

I spent vacations on Maura, during my last years at the bank, posing as Bill Montesque. They were expensive trips but a necessary investment. During my brief stays, I made it a point to establish my identity as a person who loved the Island and intended to retire there. I was accepted as a man who had suffered a horrible tragedy back in the States. I never spoke of it. Rumor had it that my whole family had been killed in the crash of my private plane. I had managed to be the source of the rumor. One night, while pretending to be drunk and in a deep depression, I gave a friendly native woman a brief capsule of the accident without mentioning facts that could be verified. My cover story, which was accepted by all, went something like this: After leaving Lockheed, where I had worked as a design engineer, I had developed a hydrogen pump that I sold to the French government for a very large sum. That left me a wealthy man.

The island was so small that it did not appear on most maps, an ideal abode for Montesque. After five years I formed close friendships with the small group of families that were the residence of the island. Their blood was a mixture of American, Australian and Japanese. Oceanographers were attracted to the island each spring, for a brief period, when the offshore waters became a whale playground. The rest of the year we were left happily alone.

There was much more cash then I expected. I actually felt a little agitated when a customer went to one of my boxes that contained cash. On my completion of the journal of safe contents, and having a key for every safe, I announced that I would take an early retirement in two months.

While the keys were accumulating, I had carefully laid out each step of my departure. The end game looked very promising. If everything went well, Bill Kias would no longer exist. Bill Montesque rested in his coffin, awaiting the rising of the moon. When it was time Montesque would come forth, being replaced by Kias in the nether world.

I knew I could still cancel the operation and avoid the possibility of spending twenty or thirty years in a very uncomfortable retirement home, but the roar of the surf on Maura was constantly ringing in my ears, drowning out any doubt of my success.

Naturally, I would have to walk out of the bank with bags of cash over my shoulder. This had to be done without anyone casting a suspicious eye.

You say preposterous. Planning my boy, planning, study the board.

I decided that four of those extra, extra-large heavy-duty bags the branch used to contain their garbage, would suffice as my coffers. On Friday, my last day, I quietly locked myself in the vault, by closing the grill gate after the bank was closed to the public. I could count on at least two undisturbed hours. Following my journal, I quickly removed the cash, placing it in the bags. I also moved tins randomly from one safe to another, keeping a record of each switch. I had a brief interruption when a co-worker, who could not make my retirement dinner, which was being held that evening, came to the main gate to say good bye.

There were some boxes I did not move. I had become, over the years, aware of serious financial problems of some of my customers. I wasn't all-bad. Like the Gotham Times, I had also compiled a "Neediest Cases" list that included customers who were down on their luck and needed a boost. I only wished I could see their faces when they opened their boxes and found them stuffed with Mr. Coffee's green beans.

I then moved the cash bags to the garbage storage area, known as the rat room, located a few feet from the vault. Garbage was not to be removed from the branch until Tuesday.

As planned, my last day fell on the Friday prior to a three-day holiday. The vault was closed on Saturday, but I would have no problem gaining access to the bank itself on the weekend. It was quite common for bank personnel to enter the branch premises, during that time, to catch up on paper work. Time locks and Burns Electric Protection safely sealed the vault until 9 o'clock Tuesday morning. The key to the door in the lobby would not be a problem. I had been given that key several years prior.

I proceeded Friday evening to my retirement dinner, to bid a fond adieu to my co-workers. I was the Guest of Honor at a bizarre farewell party for a "bank robber." Considering the effort and success of my past endeavor, I did think a celebration was in order. It did add a certain panache to the end game.

Remembering the busy day I faced on the morrow, I apologized for my early departure. My farewell speech was brief and a bit cryptic. "Who said you can't take it with you?" They knew, of course, I meant their love and affection. I was tempted to "amen" branch manager Jack Shaw's parting remark, "Bill, we will never forget you." They had given me a darn nice watch.

Saturday morning at 9 o'clock I parked my van just around the corner of the branch. I wore a Gotham Bank sweatshirt for the occasion, plus a Gotham Bank baseball hat. As usual, there were people in the lobby using our cash machines. I opened the door, placing myself in the branch proper. I brought up two bags of garbage from the rat room to alleviate any suspicion. I opened them slightly to provide the proper aroma and placed them in plain view by the door leading out of the branch. The next four bags I placed directly into my van, which was out of sight of the cash machines. One of the customers was kind enough to hold the door open for me. I then returned to place the genuine garbage in front of the building.

I immediately drove to the garage that I had been renting for the past three months in my own name. Once in the garage, I placed the money in three crates addressed to Bill Montesque, Villa Montesque, Maura Jima, Bonin Islands, via Tokyo. The crates were labeled books. I dropped the crates off at the shipping agency, using a second van rented in the name of Montesque. Returning the van, the now disguised Montesque proceeded to Kennedy where he commenced a series of hedge hopping flights to the West Coast. After spending a week in San Francisco, Montesque caught a flight to Tokyo; here he boarded the Ogasawa Maru, the bi-monthly supply ship for Maura.

My last trip to Maura was the summer prior to my retirement. While there I made the arrangements for the arrival and storage of the crates.

It was a beautiful morning when I made my joyous landfall. My friends greeted me at dockside and that night we had one hell of a party celebrating Montesque putting down his roots. I couldn't contain my exhilaration. Gad, the plan had worked without a hitch.

The supply ship from Tokyo delivered everything the island

needed, the second Monday of the month. Pacing myself carefully, I used my wealth as a tool to maintain our paradise. I, of course, had to be careful that generosity shown to my neighbors did not draw attention to our island.

I contributed a sizable amount to the building fund for our new church and medical facilities, without flaunting my fortune. My beneficence caused a movement among the small populous that I should be appointed the Administrator. I quickly quenched this idea by feigning poor health. Any picture of me appearing anywhere would only bring tears to my eyes and Mr. Coffee and the Ax-man to my beach.

I have never actually counted my booty; it was just too much. I think I overdid it. It was sizable and always growing. Occasionally I would leave the island for a trip to Tokyo. From there I would fly to my bank in Hong Kong, where large cash transactions were not questioned. Still, my financial adviser was always shocked when I would show up with large amounts of cash. He would often suggest that I make use of their safe deposit accommodations. Of course, like all scalawags, I trusted no one. I kept my main stash buried in an old cave, high up in the mountains.

My exhilaration was replaced by a strange let down. A flame deep inside of me was being quenched. I realized my great adventure was over. Kias had run with the tiger and now he was no more. It would take a while before Montesque adjusted to this new lifestyle. Surprisingly, he had no problem. Eden is Eden.

I always felt a twinge of guilt whenever Gabriella played for me. Surely, the whole world deserved to share in the pleasure of listening to an artist of such rare talent. How could one justify keeping the "Mona Lisa" in a closet? She had been constantly deluged with requests to tour the United States. She finally permitted me to convince her to accept an invitation to participate in the celebration of the one-hundredth anniversary of the Metropolitan, in Gotham City.

From the moment her ship disappeared over the horizon I was in a depressed state. I did not realize how much of me I had given her. I now knew the pain of love. I lived for the moment I could witness her performance via television. I had a satellite dish installed on the roof of the villa for just that occasion.

The grand moment finally arrived. The announcer said that over

500-million people would be able to view the concert. The stage darkened, a dim spotlight focused only on the outline of a woman playing a violin. The sound of Mendelssohn's Concerto in E Minor, for violin, penetrated the blackness of the stage. Slowly, as she played, the spotlight grew in intensity. The ravishing figure of Gabriella dressed in a stunning black-lace gown appeared, with her violin pressed to her chin. The three-movement work was being played with barely a pause between them. It was without doubt her finest performance. She never looked more exquisite, a feast for both the ear and the eye.

At the close of her performance the audience rose as one to give a crashing ovation. The cries of "Bravisima!" rang throughout the house. The stage was covered with bouquets. Violin in one hand and bow in the other, she bowed gracefully exposing the Gates necklace to 500-million viewers. I had stolen my own noose.

"LIGHTS OUT, LIGHTS OUT IN THERE!"

I can still hear the loud surf on Maura beating in my ears.

Bill Kias #P0897698 San Quentin Prison.

Platinum Premium Service & Support Policy

Dear Mr. Waygate,

I thought you would like to hear from a grateful customer how your Platinum Premium Service & Support Policy came to my aid.

I noticed recently that my Waygate Pentium was running as slow as a snail walking backwards. I had become such a joke among the 486ers that I began to shun them. My computer would be classified as new if it weren't a computer. I had paid twenty-three hundred bucks for it in May. I see now that it isn't even listed in Waygate's advertisements. Your cheapest computer is a lot faster and more powerful than mine and only twelve hundred dollars. I see you're throwing in a printer... that really hurts. The speed of advancing technology is frightening. What you invent today has to be marketed within the month. Soon you may have to date them like milk cartons. I finally figured out that the right time to buy a computer is in the future. The New York Times is spreading a vicious rumor that you are thinking about giving them away and giving AOL a run. I don't believe that for a moment.

Luckily, knowing nothing is perfect, I paid extra for your Platinum Premium Service & Support Policy. I wanted to be guaranteed the very best of support.

Seeing "Old Bess" had started to drag, I immediately took advantage of my Platinum Premium Service & Support Policy, in order that she might regain her youth. My only concern was how long it would take your repairman to come to my home.

Charley, a technician in North Dakota answered my phone call and I explained the problem.

"Bill, you have a virus that has destroyed a part of your conventional memory." I quickly denied his accusation, telling him I had always used protection. Norton's Anti-Virus was constantly on guard. He kept insisting it was a virus. I felt like a nice girl accused of being the East Coast distributor of a venereal disease.

He spent the first hour giving me tons of instructions and having me push every combination of keys on the keyboard. Charley was about as patient and as persistent as you can get. He finally gave up on the idea of a virus.

"Charley, don't waste your time. Just send out the repairman. I have the Platinum Premium Service & Support Policy," I said.

There was a long pause. Finally, I again heard the voice from North Dakota. "Bill, do you have a Philips-head screwdriver, tweezers and a needle-nose handy? We are going to have to go in."

I thought only surgeons used that language to one another. What in hell does he mean "we"?

"I want you to take the case off the tower, go in, and move some parts around."

"Charley, I get nervous when I wind my watch."

"Don't worry about it."

I thought, "A six-month-old $2,300 computer is going to have it's guts switched around by a guy who puts his finger in his ear when he tries to pick his nose?"

Taking the cover off the tower was not tough. That's what I would like to say, but for me it was tough. The second and third hour was spent taking "Old Bess" apart.

"Case off."

"Do you see the battery in the corner?"

"I see nothing that looks like a battery," I said.

"That round disk in the corner."

Long pause. Finally, I respond, "is it about the size of a nickel?"

"Yea. Do you see that set of...?" (God knows what he said.) "I want you to move the jumper off the second of the third set of..."(?) "About three inches from the nickel."

"What's a jumper?"

"That's what's connecting them," Charley responded.

Long pause. "Charley, I think I see those things." There was a whole bunch of little things that were about three thousands of an inch wide, in sets of three and four. Some of them were connected to each other by these tiny, tiny things he called jumpers. By now I have my trusty magnifying glass in hand and my arthritic spine is killing me. I go nose to nose with the jumpers.

"Bill, I want you to take the jumper off of S3 and S4 and put it on S2 and S3."

"What do you mean S3 and S4 and S2 and S3? What the hell do you mean; there is about a hundred of them?"

"Each one has a number on it."

"You're kidding," I insisted. Sure enough, I peruse them with the glass and they are numbered. Talk about a prayer on a head of a pin. I'm talking about parts that I can only see with a magnifying glass. I am in the heartland of the microprocessor.

Now the impossible starts. I have to pull a jumper off and attach it to S2 and S3. To really appreciate my task, you have to see a jumper. Look at this one. (.) Using the needle-nose to get a hold of a jumper is like trying to pick up a grain of sand with the bucket of a steam shovel.

I struggle and struggle. My right thumb, damaged in an accident, is near useless. I keep thinking; if I ever do get this damn thing off, I'm sure in hell going to drop it into that maze of the microscopic, and how would I ever be able to face Charley?

I soon realize moving a jumper requires the hand of a female violinist with the nerves of a person who has been dead a week. I reach into the very depths of my faith and beg God for a steady hand. The jumper is soon submerged in a drop of sweat from my nose. It takes forever and forever, but I do it.

After accomplishing my mission, I reconnect all the plugs into the back.

During this whole operation the phone line has been open. It has taken so long that Charley has had his Platinum Premium Service & Support Policy lunch. I am exhausted, my suspenders are soaked with sweat, and my back is killing me.

"Hey, Charley, what did you have for lunch? Sounds pretty good. I'm starving. Okay, Charley, switch on."

We booted it up for about thirty seconds to a minute.

"Okay, Bill, shut it down. I want you to strip it down again and put the jumper in its original position."

In the pause that followed you could have built a pyramid and gotten a good start on a second.

Finally, Charley spoke up. He is a real cool guy. "Bill, I've got plenty of time. Just be careful to put the jumper back exactly where you had it. You don't want to blow the motherboard."

"Charley, are you sure you have plenty of time?"

"Bill, I'm with you until the job is done. You have the Platinum Premium Service & Support Policy. No problem."

I had a strange feeling that Charley had a big grin on his face.

"That's great, Charley. Listen Charley. Moving that jumper took a lot out me. Besides that, I think I was lucky as hell. I'm not as nimble as I used to be. You will have to bear with me, I'm on in years; just hit 92," I lied. "I'm missing a thumb on my right hand. The other problem is I have to hold my right hand with my left to stop it from shaking. Stay next to that phone, Charley, I'll be needing your support."

I then went into my kitchen and had my Platinum Premium Service & Support Policy lunch. There was no need to hurry; Charley had plenty of time. I started the meal off with a Manhattan followed by a well-cooked cheeseburger. I always noticed that after a second Manhattan there was no need for me to hold my right hand with my left. I almost forgot that Charley was on the phone.

After a leisurely lunch and a glance at the newspaper I picked up the phone again. "Hey, Charley. I had a delicious lunch and now I'm going to get hot on that jumper." I went back to "Old Bess" and replaced the jumper without hearing an explosion. I guess I didn't blow the motherboard, whatever the hell that means. "Charley, the jumper is back in its original position."

"Bill, push the button."

"Old Bess" came flashing on at top speed.

May I suggest, Mr. Waygate that you include with your Platinum Premium Service & Support Policy one packet containing:

1-Philips-head screwdriver,

1-Tweezers,

1-Needle-nose Pliers,

1-Magnifying glass,

2-Manhattans, very dry.

Yours truly,
Bill Monks

Panic

I do not take to flying and would even prefer being shorter. I hate flying. I'm scared stiff of flying. My wife Dorothy and I booked on to the American Eagle Line for a flight to Washington, DC, out of Kennedy. I had failed at every attempt to miss my son's graduation.

Dot and I sat in the terminal at Kennedy watching passengers walking down these tunnels and going directly on to their planes. I thought it was a marvelous idea. Who the heck wants to see the machine that was going to mangle them?

Suddenly some girl is parading around the terminal saying "American Eagle, American Eagle, please follow me."

Sure enough we follow her out onto the field. It seemed like a half a mile. There, sitting on the tarmac, in the middle of nowhere, is a tiny, tiny plane. I guess there was about eight of us who were boarding it. I can't believe that we are getting into this toy. I expect to see the plane drawing its power from a rubber band stretching down the isle. How come everybody else has a huge plane?

The lady who brought us to the plane chickens out. She locks the hatch and says, "Have a pleasant flight," before she beats it. That is an oxymoron of the first order.

As we taxied for the take off, I kept saying to myself, "Too many passengers, much too many."

My wife was sitting there opening up a book.

Then all of a sudden the plane stops. It didn't catch on fire or blow up. It was worse than that; it was the beginning of a slow death. The pilot announces there will be a short delay; we have to stop for another passenger.

I looked out the window and I first thought three guys were trying to sneak on by paying for one ticket and sharing one suit. If it were a skit on TV you would have died laughing, but this was real life. It looked as if it was something Candid Camera had rigged up for laughs. Our new passenger was one of those poor unfortunates who must have weighed in at five hundred pounds. Gad, he was big and round. He had a hell of a tough time getting on the plane and couldn't get down the aisle. They put him on a bench in the front of the plane. There was no way we were going to get off the ground.

What did they do when a guy swam up to one of the Titanic's over crowded lifeboats? They hit him on the head with an oar and nobody thought anything of it. Thinking of the women and children, I think they should kick him the hell out now. At least we could put it to a vote. No doubt the whole thing was planned. If he were the first guy on the plane, he would have been flying solo.

My wife kept reading her book. I immediately went deep into prayer. I was hoping we would hedgehop to DC, staying as close to the ground as possible. I didn't look out the window. The motor seemed to sputter during the whole flight. I had an awful feeling that due to our extreme weight we were consuming much too much gas. We were traveling at an extremely low speed. At times I believe we were motionless, about to fall like a stone. Somebody had to do something. The fat guy knew what he was getting into when he got on. I decided, for the good of all, I was going to ask him to jump.

Just at the moment I was rising from my seat the pilot ordered us to fasten our seat belts for the landing. After we had landed, I was really surprised that the rest of the passengers seemed to be unaware of the close call. Let me tell you; that was close.

The Hat

Even though I had retired from Citibank, it was to my advantage not to remove my account. I found that even though the Bank was in Manhattan, my computer was able to ford the Hudson at will. I was able to do 90% of my bill paying and banking in the comfort of my home.

Only on rare occasion would I travel to New York to deposit checks. Today was one of those days where I had to actually bus it to the Port Authority terminal and then walk to a nearby Citibank Branch. I didn't mind. I knew I would be back in an hour.

As I walked into the vestibule of the Branch, I found it to be almost empty. There were the 30 or so Automatic Teller Machines that were not being used. The only occupant was a beautiful red-head, who wore a nameplate with a Citibank logo. I'm talking knock-out beauty, not 9 or 10; I'm talking big numbers. The kind of beauty that would make Higgins stutter. This was tall, pedestal material. She was at that age that only women know and men couldn't care less.

She approached me and offered her services. I declined her kind offer and said that I just wanted to slip a checking deposit envelope into an ATM machine. She insisted on helping me make the simple transaction. She told me she was stationed in the vestibule to enlist customers to take part in our computer banking system.

As she starts her sales pitch on computer banking I cut her short, fool that I am, and I inform her that I am already a participant. She immediately tacks and starts asking me my opinion of this new system.

She is startled when I mention that my home is in Fairview. It turns out that she had grown up in my town and attended the local grammar and high school. Her parents now live elsewhere, but they still visit our famous pasta shop. She tells me the banking job is just filler and that her real occupation is acting. This news does not surprise me. She is not only stunning, but she is emoting as if she had been standing there, waiting for my arrival.

There is no doubt that she is dedicated to her profession, and really enjoys talking about it. She tacks again, leaving banking far to stern, and with very little prodding tells me of her experiences on the stage.

Due to a life long yearning to be an actor, I have always been drawn to the theatrical page. I find myself telling her my thoughts on the theater. We go heavy into Eugene O'Neill, whose works I have always admired. She in turn tells me what wonderful taste I have, and that she too adores O'Neill. The night before she had attended "Master Class" with Zoe Caldwell, playing Maria Callas. I had just read the reviews the previous day and it appeared to be a smash hit. For some strange reason she is not suggesting that I see it, but insisting.

It appears that she has enjoyed some reasonable success in the theater, and shares with me the pain of being separated from her boyfriend, who is also pursuing an acting career in California.

I find our little chat delightful. As she talked, and talk freely she did, I found her captivating. The bank had disappeared; we were alone. This ravishing beauty is sharing her hopes and dreams with me. It has not been always so. I find I'm in the company of Violetta. Can Giorgio be far behind? I am standing on unholy ground. I feel a strange bonding taking place. This is madness! She is telling me how fascinating she finds me. If she mentions my blue eyes, I know I am going to wake up.

Then again there our some things you just don't lose. They say charm and magnetism are buried with you. I find the years slipping away; I can feel my hair turning ebony. I recall Paul Newman, now 74, did all right with the ladies in his last picture.

As we discuss "Masterclass", I tell her of my newfound love of opera. There is no doubt that she is enthralled. Her green eyes are all mine.

Do my eyes deceive me, do I see a slight hint of worship, or is she blowing smoke at me? Do I sense a little snow in the air?

While I'm thinking of how much money I have in my account, and how far we could get on it, I had not noticed that we were no longer alone, several customers were using the ATMs. Feeling a sense of guilt at monopolizing her time, I attempt to break off the conversation. She reaches out to lightly hold my hand. Strange, but I feel certain she does not want me to leave. I tell her I must leave, and as we part we exchange names. She reminds me that she has a bit part in the upcoming production, "Casino", and hopes some day to meet me in the pasta shop.

I return to the Bus Terminal in a state of euphoria. My sciatic limp has developed a certain spring to it. What did this beautiful captivating woman see in this old man of three score ten? There is just no accounting for the eye of the beholder.

I return home and entered my den to mull over that heavenly morning. Perhaps a little La Traviata and a chilled Manhattan are called for. My mulling is brought up short as I remove my cap. The words embroidered on the face of it catch my eye. The cap had been a gift from my daughter Joanne, when she had returned from a recent trip to California. The logo and the gold lettering were quite ornate. Above the peak of the cap and inside a fancy embroidered marquee were printed the words "UNIVERSAL STUDIOS", underneath in gold script, "Hollywood". I collapsed in a fit of pain and laughter. Who said, "to live it again is past all endeavor?" For a few moments I had been back under the palm trees and they seemed to be swaying.

Mom Was a Marine

Each morning on the way to James Madison High School, Pep and I would pass the draft board. There would always be either a friend or a relative hanging out in front, waiting to be processed. It was like a giant drain sucking all the men out of the neighborhood.

When we graduated in January of '44, we were still seventeen and too young for the draft. Phil had already left for flight school and Harry was being trained as a radioman for a Navy Avenger. My two brothers had also left, Bob to the Air Corps, and Dick to the Navy.

After graduation, Pep and I worked in the A&S Department Store for about four months as stock boys. When I got my "Greetings From The President" (draft notice), we both quit. We got one heck of a lecture in the personnel office, by a somber old gentleman wearing a black suit. He spoke to us about the importance of business ethics and our responsibility to our employer.

"The proper thing to do was to provide the firm two weeks notice before resigning," he said. "What you fellows are doing is just not done." It certainly made a lot of sense. We hung our heads while we listened, felt very guilty, apologized, then we quit.

Pep got his "greetings" shortly thereafter. We had our eighteenth birthday two weeks apart. One week later Uncle Sam gave us a choice of services. Pep chose the Navy and I went to Parris Island, the Boot Camp for all Marines east of the Mississippi. I was about to spend the hottest summer in the history of South Carolina learning how to obey an order and to stay in back of the guy in front of me.

It was a traumatic experience leaving Brooklyn, with a group of strangers, for an unfamiliar destination. Most of us, no doubt, were sharing the same feeling. As the train headed south we started to lighten up and get acquainted. By the time we reached Washington, a lot of sharing had taken place ,and close friendships were developing. As the train reached South Carolina, the guys in the car had bonded into a bunch that appeared to be bound for a Giant football game.

Crossing over the bridge to Parris Island was a one way trip. A meat cleaver was about to sever any ties and relationships with family and friends. Nothing again would ever be the same. Parris Island licked her lips; she fed on innocence.

When our bus arrived, a large Marine Corporal greeted us. He was about thirty, huge and very broad. He was poured into a tailored uniform with two stripes on his creased sleeve. The man was extremely ugly; under his slanting forehead he had predatory, ebony eyes, sunk deep into his face. Under his left eye a large scar pulled his cheek into a permanent scowl. It was a cruel face that did not hide the obvious contempt for us. For a long while he just stood at the edge of the group, staring at us, not saying a word.

In a moment we were aware of his presence and all conversation ceased. You could sense fear building up in the group. There were sixty of us, a majority being eighteen-year-olds. There were a few guys from 25 to 32, who had avoided the draft till now. The Government was scraping the barrel.

I guess, just to break the silence, our ROTC man spoke up. He had slight military training at NYU. "Where can we wash up?" That was a big mistake.

There was a long pause. The behemoth ignored our man. I heard my first southern accent. "My name is Corporal Stone. I am your Drill Instructor. You will always, always address me as Sir. Where in hell did you guys come from? Goddamn zoot suit Yankees—peg pants and long hair. How in hell did you clowns get in here? MOVE IT, SHITBIRDS! FOUR RANKS OF 15! NOW!"

I thought the name "shitbirds" was rather repugnant. That is the only name used for a Boot on Parris Island. We had fallen into the hands of one angry man. After a confusing muddle, we slowly formed into four ranks. Again he stood there glaring at us, with a face that cried out for a banana.

He finally exploded, vilifying us as a group, using all sorts of profanity; every noun he used was having sexual relations. We could not understand his behavior. Why was he mad at us? Suddenly he started picking individuals from the ranks for personal attention. He started with R.O.T.C. He destroyed him with demeaning comments about his mother, father, and the girl back home. Nobody really liked

ROTC's attitude during the trip. He had a four-star general way about him. If the Drill Instructor hadn't looked so formidably evil, we would have collapsed laughing. He was not destroying R.O.T.C in order to entertain us. Stone was really sick and to be taken seriously. He seemed to be barely containing an urge to do us bodily harm.

His harangue boiled down to, "You are mine! Forget about Mom. I'm your Mother now and I'm going to tuck you shitbirds in from today until Aug 15th. You have just made the biggest mistake of your life! You have met me! You are in hell! If you can stand the heat, you will be a Marine, and you will stand the heat!" I later realized that he had either lied to us or he had one hell of tough Mother. He must have been a product of a broken, gorilla family.

I soon noticed the poor man had a hearing problem. He would stand with his nose almost touching mine and inform me that he couldn't hear me, forcing me to shout into his face. He loved being called Sir. I had no problem hearing him. I guess he had to shout to hear himself. His memory was shot too; he couldn't remember names. He called everybody that same repugnant name. It was my first encounter with a real live son-of-a-bitch.

You think I'm snowing you. My friend, there is a whole new life out there that you don't want to know about. Life on Parris Island is one big boil on your rear end.

After are heads were shaved, we were given tan pith helmets, green dungarees and heavy boondockers (shoes). The sixty free-spirits that had entered P.I. had become sixty scared, bald, look-a-likes. Something horrible was happening; I was losing my identity. We were helpless, in the hands of a mad man who actually hated us.

From my first moment on P.I., we were totally immersed in a training program that used our every breath for the good of the Corps. Our schedule was extremely compact; individual time and privacy no longer existed. Whatever they were doing to us, they had it down to a science. We soon realized that the ultimate goal of the training was to destroy the self, kill the individual. The military instruction was secondary to mind control.

All the Corps wanted was raw meat. Life was to be found only in the group. We were to exist only as a cell in the body. A lobotomy was thrown in with the hair cut; all free will was removed. A mental gang rape in reverse was part of the training program. The group would think as one, and of only one thing: "OBEY WITHOUT QUESTION."

I wondered how anybody could live in South Carolina while enduring that horrible heat. Every day in the sun it was well over a hundred degrees. June, July, and August of that year were the hottest summer South Carolina ever had. I would watch the uniform of Bill Farrell, the man in front of me, turn from light green to black as we marched; beads of sweat would drop off his ears. We popped salt tablets like peanuts.

So many guys were collapsing that an order came down that if the temperature went over 95, we were not to go on the drill field. Our Drill Instructor just scoffed and we continued drilling in the sand between the barracks.

The DI had a thing about keeping in step and rank while we threw our rifles from one shoulder to the other. We would practice this close order drill for hours, on a field of deep, loose, burning sand. God it was hot. He would march beside us constantly repeating "Reep, Reep, Reep." I could never figure out what he was trying to tell us.

Moe Kershoff was the first man to collapse; down he went into the hot sand. He was a big, fat, soft guy from Brooklyn. He must have come in at 250. I don't think Moe ever exercised in his life. As we marched over him, we naturally went out of step to avoid hurting him. After we passed over him, the DI gave the order "To the rear, march." Back we went every man in step. As we approached our fallen comrade, lying where he fell, we were told that there was a possibility of stepping on him, or over him, depending where your foot fell, but you kept in STEP and in RANK.

"The man who goes out of step or breaks rank will take that shitbird's place and we will walk over you." Stone was always serious about keeping in step. I imagine he thought it looked pretty. Well, we marched over him. We did our best not to step on him. Moe later joined us back at the barracks. The sand had clung to the sweat on his face and his wet uniform. He looked as if he had stepped out of his grave.

Moe was definitely a DI's nightmare: overweight, misfit, and a real blob. Even though he was in sad shape and made a lousy appearance, Moe had guts. Life on Parris Island was a chore for all of us, but for Moe the physical training was hell turned up. His special cross was made of fat. Most of Moe made it through P.I., but about 40% of him dripped on to that hot skillet. No doubt his mind was busted when we graduated, but he did look great. His family must have been flabbergasted when he came home from Boot, never believing his tale of woe. I don't think you can relate what happened down there without breaking into possessed laughter.

Each morning after calisthenics, they would pair the Boots off, in order that we might box. The matches would be fought in cold blood, with no animosity felt toward your opponent. The fight could not cease until the crimson flowed. Corp. Stone would always attempt to match two buddies. Those matches were unholy. After a match you would have a difficult time looking your opponent in the eye.

Before dawn we would fall in at attention at the foot of our sacks. Guys would collapse, like trees falling, never bending their knees. You would hear this sickening slap, as if a board fell.

You would always hesitate falling out for sick call. There was the chance they would put you in the hospital and you would lose your platoon, which meant additional time on the Island. I remember one night helping a buddy, John Cook, over to the head (bathroom) to soak the huge blisters on his feet. While we were there I made the mistake of asking a Marine, who was stepping out of the shower, for the time. I called him Joe, for lack of a name, which turned out to be a huge mistake. Joe turned out to be a nude DI. He reamed us out, leaving us at attention as he disappeared into the night. John and I didn't know what in hell to do. We finally worked up enough courage to take off, back to our barracks. I never did get the gentleman's name. Joe is probably still laughing.

Constant fatigue was always a problem, not enough sleep time. I remember standing exhausted, in front of Corp. Stone, while I attended one of his many lectures. Picture Arnold Schwarzenegger with the head of a gorilla. I was not comfortable in his company. I would go as far as saying that I was scared stiff of him. I couldn't picture him associating with human beings. That spark of humanity that each man has was long quenched, if ever lit.

God was I tired. While he talked I was having a serious problem keeping my upper lids from touching my bottom lids. The behemoth's gaze froze on me and I knew there was something horrible about to happen. My eyelids turned to lead. He was kind enough to notice my unintentional faux pas, as I went off to sleep on my feet. He had a ready remedy for my unpardonable behavior. He grabbed me by the collar with those huge hands and shook my eyeballs. I was suddenly wide-awake; my eyelids felt like feathers. I was now able to give him my complete attention. It was obvious that he had a medical background, probably specialized in narcolepsy. It was a lasting cure. To this day, I sleep with one eye open.

The only saving grace was that we were all in it together. We bonded like a herd of musk oxen. All I knew was that each day I was losing something; part of me was dying. It was as if I was bleeding "me." There was just Stone and the Platoon. I was disappearing into the system. The method the Corps used to destroy the "self" seemed so irrational. It was like punishing the man before he committed the crime. It was hard for us to fathom why they were so cruel. The system called for some constructive criticism. On second thought, I decided to wait until I got off the Island. I didn't want to put the DI's foot in my mouth.

I felt sorry for the 32 years old guys in the Platoon. It was a tough age to be made over, most of them were badly out of shape. There was no doubt that Mom had his work cut out. How do you turn a quiet family man into a ruthless killer? You teach him to hate.

Whenever we screwed up we would have the bucket drill. We really didn't have to screw up. Mom would come back to the barracks in the middle of the night; half smashed, looking like the monster after the fire. He would stand in the doorway and at the top of his lungs order "BUCKET DRILL, HIT THE DECK." Upon hearing that dreaded order you would leave a coma like sleep and leap from your sack. Eyes straining to stay open, you would place yourself at rigid attention in your skivvies at the foot of your double-decker. At the order of "Bucket" you would place your large, heavy cast iron wash bucket over your head and remain at attention. Immediately next to you is the man you share the double-decker with. Our heads were in the buckets about six inches from the metal bar that runs along the foot of the top sack. The DI, walking with the silence of a cat, would proceed down the long aisle between the two rows of bucketed Marines. You could hear the cry of pain as Stone would randomly slam a bucket into the metal bar. You would try to anticipate your bell being rung by trying to spot the toe of his shoe as he stood in front of you, giving you time to brace and cringe.

Now the bucket drill begins. Picture fifteen double deck sacks on each side of the aisle with two bucket-heads standing at the foot of each sack. On the word "GO", the first man crawls on the floor under the first double-decker, he then proceeds to climb over the top of the second double-decker, and then under the bottom of the third, etc. At his heels there are 59 other guys following the same course. Naturally the buckets remain on our heads during the whole drill; Stone keeps the herd at a fast pace with the aid of his swagger stick. It always was hilarious; the buckets were filled with cries of pain and hysterical laughter. It was all that bad, but it was the only privacy we ever had.

On Sunday afternoon, Stone attempts to walk on his hands during a break. Like a real smart-ass, I walk down the few steps that led out of the barracks on my hands to show up the DI. He pretends not to notice. The next day he shows how much he appreciated my agility.

At the rifle range you would not only learn how to fire your weapon with expertise, but you would also have to spend time on butt detail. This entails standing in a trench as the firing line places shots in a target a few feet above your head. After the firing ceases, you lower the target by sliding it down on a frame,

Down in the butts, the activity is fast moving. Targets must be disked, marked and pasted up carefully and quickly. You immediately place markers in the bullet holes, to indicate the hits. Now up go the marker poles to give the score. Maintaining that fast pace in the scorching sun is extremely difficult. It could have been worse and it was. Stone, sitting on a bench in back of me, amused himself by constantly prodding me in the back with a marker pole. My old Mom never did that. Then again, she could walk on her hands.

The Sunday of the last week of training, Farrell lit out to Post Exchange to buy a 1/2-gallon of ice cream. The DI caught him and tied the container to the top of his head, upside down. He then placed him in front of the barrack, where it was at least 110 in the sun. The platoon was ordered to fall in to witness the meltdown. In the beginning we thought it amusing...Then the sandflies came.

On graduation day, we were finally paid. Stone gave a touching speech, explaining why he had to be the monster he was. He then proceeded to remove his pith helmet and had us pass it through the ranks. Mother shook us down.

I would have been disappointed if he didn't. I was no longer innocent or naïve. I was never going back over that bridge.

It's strange how, whenever Marines meet in a small group, it's usually Parris Island, and not the campaigns, which always become the center of the conversation. Laughter always seems to drown out the wild tales of horror, as they play the game of "let me tell you about the joker we had." This guy would make us put our cast iron wash buckets over our heads. You know, I really think he got me through it. My poor bastard got it the first morning on Iwo. He wasn't a son-of-a-bitch, he was a Marine.

The Death of an Eagle

It was one of those nights that you want to lock on to. It was Christmas night; we had just finished a fantastic dinner. My wife and I retired to the family room to enjoy the beauty of the burning logs. As I sat down with a Manhattan in hand, Dot came over and sat on my lap. I knew after three score ten that it doesn't get any better than this.

The grandchildren were deep into their new toys and frolicked on the tufted rug. Please, dear God, don't let them knock over the tree. With fifteen grandchildren, twelve of them under eight years, I definitely need a bigger family room

My seven kids were still sitting at the table talking over their coffee. Two of the girls were lawyers, and from what I could hear, they were expounding on the joy of their clients inheriting fortunes. Jack, my youngest boy, yelled out to me, "Hey, Dad, did anybody ever die and leave you something?"

"Yes son, about fifty years ago an eagle died, and left me a fortune."

"What did you do with it Dad?"

I smiled. " I still have it."

The kids laughed and went back to their chatter. Who could figure Dad?

My thoughts drifted back to the long ago, the night of my inheritance. It was night, only it wasn't night. The busting of shells and flares kept the sky a bright orange. The light reflected back down off the cloud of smoke that encapsulated the island of Iwo Jima. The ground was covered with what seemed like a dense fog, only it wasn't fog. Thick vapor choked the lungs as the acrid fumes of sulfur seeped out of the pits. Hell was loose. It had escaped earth's bondage.

Grotesque bodies lay over the landscape, some partially covered by the black sand. The scene of carnage could only be compared to the last level of Dante's inferno.

I hunkered down for the night, praying, constantly praying. The roar of shells never ending, there was no room for silence. I felt an unbelievable emptiness. They were all dead or wounded: Frenchy, Nose, Kilpatrick, the whole damn squad. I was dead; nothing left but a bag of skin.

"Look out Joe, coming in. Move your gear. I just joined your squad."

I quickly move my pack and cartridge belt as this young kid jumps into my hole. He was a kid. Couldn't have been more than 18 and 140 pounds. I said to myself, "this kid thinks the coach sent him off the bench to join the game. He was actually happy to be here. Eighteen-year-olds don't die."

I said to him, "Where did you come from?"

"I'm a replacement off the Funston. We have been out there circling the island for three days... what a show! Now they got the ship packed with wounded. Fifty of us just joined Charlie Company. You must have taken some losses."

"Yea, kid, we took our share. Charlie had 250 when we came ashore. There are only about 40 of us left. Just sit real still kid, and welcome to hell. Geez kid, when did you get out of Boot?"

"About three month ago."

He suggests that we make the hole bigger. I explain two good reasons why we can't. "One you can't dig in this sand and the other is that you will get killed before you got your shovel off your pack."

That night the kid kept talking. He came from a turkey farm outside of Cedar City, Utah. I really wasn't listening, I was thinking of the letter in my pack. The night before, checking the odds of getting off the island, I wrote a letter to my wife and the kids. It was a letter that I prayed my wife would never read.

As the kid rambled, the idea struck me to give him the letter. The steel downpour was tearing the hell out of the bodies. There was a good chance that if I went down, the letter would be destroyed. I figured I could use the kid as my mailbox. It was some sort of insurance. If he went down first, I would take the letter back.

I got the letter out of my pack and explained to the kid how I would appreciate it if he would carry it for me. The kid was eighteen; it never occurred to him that he was old enough to die, and that he might get hit before me.

As the hours pass, I kind of opened up. I tell him about Dot and the kids: Andy and Megan. I flash the pictures I keep in my helmet. For a moment I'm off the island as I babble about the children.

The kids all right, but he is so damn young. I can't believe there is a very good chance that he will be dead tomorrow. The kid still doesn't realize where he is.

Son-of-a-bitch, a grenade is in the hole. One of our little brown brothers has lobbed a grenade right in on us. It landed smack between us.

I freeze and the kid yells, "I got it." He throws himself on it and snuggles up to that grenade like it's his teddy bear. He takes the full force of it, tearing him to pieces. I wake up as they carry me aboard the Hospital ship.

Shortly after I get home, I receive a letter from his folks. Somehow they got the letter I had written to my wife. I go out to the turkey farm and have a sit down with the family. It was the least I could do, but it was the hardest thing I ever did.

They show me the family album; he seems to be on every page. One picture shows the kid in a Boy Scout uniform. His chest is covered with merit badges. He didn't look any older in the hole. His Dad stares at the picture "My boy was an Eagle, the highest rank you can get in Scouting. Come into the living room, we want to show you what the Government gave our boy."

I suspected what they were about to show me. I remembered our Colonel wrote up the report about what happened that night. There it was. The biggest merit badge of all, the Congressional Medal of Honor. They want me to stay the night but I just can't do it. I keep hearing the kid saying, "I got it."

Did I ever inherit anything? The kid left me everything.

One Half Hour 'til Closing

Bruce J. Killdare
President & CEO
Fairview Medical Center
7600 Lake Road,
South Bergen, NJ 07047

Dear Bruce:

I was grateful to receive your letter asking for a donation to your emergency department. I am also glad to hear of the plans for the expansion of your new waiting area. I, for one, can testify for the need for this expansion. By my own experience, I would say that room could not be big enough. Let me go into a little detail. Possibly you could use my testimony, to add to Maria's and John's, as an aid to your fund drive.

I was about 62 years old at the time of my accident. I had taken a rather bad fall on my bike in Hudson County Park. The damage to my body was quite life threatening. I broke most of the ribs on my right side causing severe punctures in my lung. My clavicle was broken, which not only left me with a large hump on what remains of my shoulder, but also with severe nerve damage, which caused the loss of the use of my thumb. My thumb now points at a right angle to my hand; this makes it very difficult to hitchhike in a straight line.

The police called an ambulance and within a very short time my stretcher was deposited on the floor of your emergency room. As I lay there waiting for assistance, I thought how odd life was. Six days previously I had watched the TV program, 60 Minutes, where they discussed the lack of speed in the care of trauma cases in the emergency room. They made a strong point of impressing upon the viewer the chances of the trauma patient dying, if he did not receive immediate care within the first half-hour of his arrival.

As I lay there for about ten minutes I reviewed the program in my mind (I had nothing else to do). I thought, wouldn't it be nice if someone came along and gave me some succor. After another 15 minutes went by, I noticed that one of my ambulance attendants was losing his nerve. He kept asking, "Where is the doctor? Where is the doctor? This guy is going into shock."

Those last few words recalled Mike Wallace's admonition that trauma usually led to shock, which led to seeing that bright light at the end of the tunnel. As my allotted 1/2-hour was running out, I remember saying to myself "Bill, shock is the last place you want to go." I was thinking of how do you avoid it and what the hell is it?

Now there are two or three people yelling, "Where is the Doctor? What the hell is keeping him? Why doesn't he come?"

Ah! Someone sees the doctor coming. Everything is right with the world. The White Knight approaches amidst the sighs of my surrounding entourage. All I can see of my savior is his legs, as he passes me by, to pick up a phone on the wall about three feet from where I'm lying. Hell, he's making up for lost time. He is probably calling for a specialist. God bless him; all is forgiven.

The phone is so close I can hear his conversation, and so can the two or three attendants I have near me.

Much to my disappointment and surprise he is not calling a specialist, but his stockbroker. We all listen as the White Knight advises his broker in great detail to make several stock transactions for him. I can still remember the comment of an innocent and naive nurse. "I DON'T BELIEVE THIS."

He finally hangs up, looks down at the form gasping for breath at his feet, and casually remarks something like, "Put him in ICU and I'll put a tube in his chest," before he meanders on.

Thanks to Mike's warning about shock and my desire to someday come back and kill that S.O.B., I did not die.

It was on a Friday in October, 1987. The market crashed that day. Every night I still remember him in my prayers. I pray that he was buying.

When I got up to ICU, the farce continued. A nurse actually punched me. She was pushing me on my broken side to get me on a gurney. After begging her to remove her hands from my side, I dug my nails into her hand, (a reflex action) to protect myself from the excruciating pain. She was rather a large blond and had a couple of pounds on me. She cursed me and delivered a resounding thump to my poor, pain-racked body. She obviously had reflexes too. You had to be there to enjoy it.

After what seemed about six trips to X-ray (I lost count), you didn't seem to know what else to do with me. Citibank doctors couldn't believe I was X-rayed that many times. I think I hold the record in your hospital. You should check it out.

You didn't seem to have any treatment for what ailed me. You did give me a little blue sling for my arm to rest in, plus the tube in my chest, and then placed me out on the ward.

After leaving ICU, I was placed under the care of a nurse who had approximately 14 to 16 other patients to take care of. Luckily my oldest son was present when I started to hemorrhage. He is a tough F.B.I. man, but it kind of shook him up to see his father belching out blood on the floor. He helped me to a standing position in order that I might not drown in my own blood. I had a good size puddle at my feet before any staff arrived. One thing I'll never forgive your hospital for is that pained look on my son's face as he was watching helplessly, as the blood gushed out of my mouth. I don't know what caused me the most anxiety, spewing the blood or having to watch the pain on my son's face.

Bill and I put on quite a show as the crowd collected. When the commotion finally died down and I was put back in ICU, I was visited by the Nurse in Charge. She seemed to be standing beside herself. She was mad as hell at me; for some strange reason she held me accountable for my bleeding and the commotion. I'll always remember that bitter look on her face and her parting words, "you scared the shit out of us." I almost said I was sorry.

Naturally, I was going to sue you but I figured your poor patients would end up paying the bill. On behalf of your patients, let me lift my voice in a resounding, "HELP!!"

As far as the care received in your Medical Center, let's just say you renewed my faith in the power of prayer.

I was a Marine during WW2 and saw the Flag go up on Surabachi, on the island of Iwo Jima. I would rather take my chances on that beach then come under your guns again.

You can use the $1,000,000 I didn't sue you for towards your new waiting room. All I ask is that you put up a bronze plaque in the memory of the guys who couldn't wait because their half-hour ran out.

Yours truly,
Bill Monks

P.S. For the care I received and the money I paid you, I would have been much better off if the ambulance had taken me to the Hotel St. Regis. They wouldn't have mended me either, but think of the service that money would buy. I priced that sling at my drug store. Next time, use my belt and save a quarter.

There Was a Little Girl

When Francine arrived at our home, she was two and a half years old. She had been removed from a family that was made up of handicapped parents and her three handicapped siblings. The other children were eventually placed in state institutions. Prior to their removal, the siblings had beat upon Francine and treated her like a rag doll. Then, for a two-year period prior to coming to our home, Francine had been placed in a substandard foster home. We could see rope burns that had become calluses on her ankles. It was obvious that she had been tied in a crib. Our family doctor said she was on the verge of starvation.

Francine was extremely small for her age, she had the appearance of a lovely, ivory cameo. In spite of her extreme delicate condition and emaciated appearance, she was a beautiful child. Her hair was silk blonde with natural waves and a curl in the middle of her forehead. Her skin was milk white, almost translucent. Her features were perfect and she had the most beautiful green eyes.

The most extraordinary factor of her condition was that the child had shut down all of her senses: hearing, seeing, touching, tasting, crying, walking, and talking; none of these signs of life were functioning. She had returned to the womb. It was hard to understand how a human being could willingly blind oneself. She refused to focus her eyes, giving her the appearance of having the glass eyes of a doll. Soon after her arrival, trying to bring life to her eyes, I bundled her up and brought her out into a heavy snowfall. She never saw a flake.

My Pastor assured himself that she was stone deaf when she seemed not to hear the pot he was banging behind her head. The only sound she emitted was a constant low moan. The child would not touch anything; her hands hung limp at her sides. She stood on her stick like legs and rocked, emitting that low moan.

The strangest manifestation of her condition was that there were no tears, she would not cry. She appeared to be a porcelain mannequin of a little girl. She made no attempt to walk or crawl. She possessed all the physical handicaps of a Helen Keller plus a determination to stay that way. Her mind would not respond to outside stimuli. She appeared to be in another dimension, a dimension we could not penetrate. Contact was impossible.

Her instinctive desire of self-preservation had forced her to flee her threatening environment. Her only defense was to flee back to the womb. She had apparently sealed herself into her strange prison. Who was this person who preferred the nether world? It was this child whose moan betrayed her pain, and yet did not cry out for help. Was there a way out of a dungeon that had neither doors nor windows? Could we bring this beautiful child back to life?

When we attempted to feed her we soon realized she would neither chew nor suck. We kept her alive by blending all sorts of highly nutritious food into a liquid and pouring it into her. She could swallow.

The first night we put her in her crib we found out the why of the rope marks. We left her standing in the crib and went downstairs. Suddenly, a loud thump, thump, thump, thump was shaking the house. We ran upstairs to find Francine clutching the side of the crib as she jumped as high as a kite. We immediately had to construct extensions on to the sides in order to contain her. Each night she jumped till she fell exhausted to sleep. She never, ever woke up at night. Of course we never would have known if she woke; she never cried.

I happened to be acquainted with a Dr. Sheinfeld, a man renowned in his field of genetics. I consulted him about her condition. He recommended that we immediately place her in an institution, basing his prognosis on the fact that she possessed no building blocks. There are some things you just can't do.

When I would come home from work I would go up to our bedroom, lie on the bed and sit this living doll on my chest. For days and weeks we went through a routine, whereby I attempted eye and ear contact. I played a tape of the soothing voices of women singing while I caressed her back and legs. If I attempted to make contact by staring or wiggling my fingers in front of her eyes, she rolled them up so that you could see only the whites. She obviously had seen enough of this world.

Her survival depended on her ability to flee this threatening unfriendly environment. I really don't remember how long this nightly routine continued but it was to no avail. However, my children spent quite an amount of time on their knees attempting to teach Francine to crawl. They succeeded and soon after she stood up and started to walk.

My kids unknowingly had opened Pandora's box and my wife, Dorothy, was about to have sainthood thrust upon her. A demon was among us posing as a beautiful, little child. She pushed anything out of the way that she could touch. This caused a large amount of breakage and spillage. Any small knick-knacks that she didn't eventually destroy in the living and dining rooms had to be placed down in the basement. Can you call a lamp a knick-knack? My wife Dorothy was speeding around the bend, under a full head of steam. Francine pulled down the drapes so often that Dorothy stopped putting them up. People knocked on the door and asked us if we were selling the house.

Then it got to the point where if you got too close to Francine, she would bite or scratch you. This usually happened when one of our seven other children approached her to show affection. It was as if we had a wild beast in the house. Every once in a while the house rang with the cry, "she got me." She kept them on their toes. She was extremely destructive; anything breakable, within her reach, was history. The only way we could react to her aggression was to sit her on the kitchen floor in a corner. She would sit, rock, and moan. She didn't display any real displeasure. That was her normal stance; isolation was her habitat.

The only things that seemed to infatuate her were curtains and women's skirts, which she never aggressively attacked. She seemed to derive pleasure by wrapping herself in the material. I presumed that there must have been a curtain near her crib in the foster home, and that a fan must have constantly put it in motion, just out of her reach. It possibly drew her attention, yet did not threaten her. In my home, my wife was not that lucky.

Francine's idea of a good time was for her and I to go to our Church about five o'clock, when it was dark and empty. I would sit on the floor behind the last pew and watch her strange behavior. She would pull and wrap herself around the sturdy drapes of the confessional. Who knows, maybe she was seeking a womb.

On one occasion while my wife and I were shopping in Macy's, my warped sense of humor overcame me. I thought, here was a wonderful opportunity to introduce Francine to some new friends. We sneaked off to where they displayed multicolored curtains on mock windows. While we strolled around I kept a pit bull grip on her. I dared not let the bull loose.

Standing in the bakery, while waiting to be served, she yanked on a woman's skirt and almost took it off. I gave the woman one of those, "What are you doing to my child?" stares.

I can not put into words the havoc she wrought at our dinner table. She had the quickest hands since Bob Cousy, the famed basketball player. She knocked over a glass or upturned a dish before the warning went from your eye to your brain. I remember one evening, after she had destroyed our dinner, I had to remove her from the table by her heels in order to protect my eyes. The whole time she showed absolutely no emotion

I'll always remember the day that the storm cloud was lifted from above our home. I was sitting in my chair in the living room enjoying my paper and sipping a soda. I was alone; it was just my shadow and me. I dropped my guard for a moment. Bingo, she nailed my soda.

Following our normal routine, without malice, I picked her up and brought her into the kitchen where I placed her in her corner. As I went back to my soggy paper, I thought I heard a cat crying. Then I accepted the impossible. I dashed into the kitchen to find that the beast had departed.

The chase had ended. The hound had its prey. There in the corner sat a little girl crying. I wanted to sit down next to her and cry with her. Tears, tears, beautiful tears. She could no longer reject love. She was giving the human race another chance.

Her first signs of recognizing me were a gentle fondling of my goatee and necktie. She was reaching out for help from that world to which she had fled. On occasion, Francine and I hiked to the top of Mount Moriah, a high hill on the outskirts of town. Here I attempted to introduce her to the beautiful world she had shut out. The view was fantastic. You could gaze across the whole state. We lay in the grass and enjoyed the solitude, only interrupted by the song of birds and drifting clouds. To catch her eye and see her smile, I plucked wild flowers to place in her lap. I blew the parachutes off the dandelion and watched them dance in the air around her. She soon learned to imitate this fine art. I'll always treasure the memory of those serene moments on Mount Moriah, where she at last flung open the door of her strange domain and bid me enter.

Call it love or bonding, we two became one. She used me as an extension of herself, a door into the world. Francine actually used my hands to pick up objects. My children said that she developed my facial expressions. My wife accused me of being the only man who gave birth.

She didn't start to speak until the age of seven. Her school had given up on her and suggested she be taught sign language. This would not have been too difficult. My in-laws are deaf and my wife signs fluently. We thought it would be better to wait. We always felt that her speech defect was due to a late maturation of the muscles of her lower jaw. I thought this also was the cause of her chewing problem. As the years went by, her pronunciation and syntax became normal. She also mastered the trick of polishing off a hero sandwich in seconds.

I think the funniest and most touching thing she ever said to me happened in a supermarket. I was chastising her rather loudly for mischievous behavior, when she pulled me down to her to whisper, "Yell in my ear, Dad." I felt like a big oaf.

"Stone walls do not a prison make."

Her first sixteen years were extremely lonely. Life in the house moved around her. Her brothers and sisters loved her but communication was difficult. Her self-imposed isolation was replaced by society's. She lacked the ability to interact socially. Often mocked and ostracized, she spent years in her room listening to music as she rocked continuously.

My heart broke when she said to me, "Dad, I need a friend."

I remember watching her approach two girls chatting on an empty beach. She stood there while they ignored her. I thought it ironic. Now we don't want you.

Francine spent most of her school time in special education classes. She didn't mainstream until she entered high school. As time passed she managed to gain the acceptance of her peers. In her junior year she was on the bowling and the volleyball teams.

While in school, it was discovered that she had a remarkable sewing talent. Our buttons popped when she won a silver and gold medal in state competition. Francine attended two proms, wearing her own beautiful dresses. I didn't feel too bad when she failed geometry. This apple didn't fall far from the tree.

She never asked for a quarter, nor was she given any. She had unbelievable pride and self esteem. Everything she ever attempted, she approached with confidence. She had as much heart and guts as any Marine I ever served with.

Francine is now 24; her hearing and eyesight are perfect. As a child her doctors predicted she would be below normal statue and sleight of frame. This is not so. Her figure is the envy of her sisters, who are no slouches in their own right. Time and maturity has only enhanced her natural beauty.

Not having love and affection during the first two years of her life should have had catastrophic effects on her long-term future development. Praise God, by some miracle, Francine has generated the ability to love and to trust. Without these virtues there is no life. In spite of the many handicaps she had to overcome, a very unique personality has emerged. Francine is now working and supporting herself. Recently she gave her Dad a break and purchased her own computer. At the present moment, with the aid of her computer, she is engaged in about thirty chess games with opponents from all over the world. Two of her opponents are college professors, another a M.D.

Quite often we pass the time playing chess. As a wood pusher, she is a worthy opponent. I have always enjoyed our games. She plays the game the way she lives her life; she cannot except defeat and would never think of resigning. She has to hear the word "mate". I win my share, but she kills me with that darn time clock. When the old man forgets to hit that clock she just sits there and smiles.

She is extremely pleasant and has that rare virtue of innocence. Her older sisters were always very popular, with steady boyfriends. Our poor butterfly was always asking me when she would meet her Mr. Right. It was a very painful period in her life. Mr. Right never came. Mr. Perfect came in his place.

He far exceeded her prayers. Billy Bud Lives. Norman is the only person I ever met whose life is based on agape love. He loves all without expecting anything in return. Everyone who meets him feels compelled to respond to his love. I have never met a better man. It's as if he was behind the door when original sin was passed out. He is what we all were supposed to be, in the beginning. When you are in his presence, a strange feeling comes over you. You are aware that you are not what you should be.

This story was written at the request of that little girl who had a little curl right in the middle of her forehead. When she was good, she was very, very good. When she was bad, she was horrid.

Go Fly a Kite

Brooklyn, N.Y. 1930-. The family came down from Boston in 1928. We purchased a new home in what was to be called Marine Park. I was sitting on the steps of my front porch with two newfound friends. We soon discovered that we had three things in common: we were all named Bill, four years old, and not allowed to cross the street. Bill Phillips (Phil) and Bill Horohoe (Harry) and I shared a lot of life. I managed to keep a close friendship with Phil until his death at 56. I am still in close touch with Harry after 66 years.

Mrs. Horohoe was a wonderful woman, but she worried and always kept a close watch on Harry. This tight rein caused Harry to miss a lot of adventure in the remote parts of the neighborhood. Those early years tried Harry's patience. He had to watch as Phil and I broke loose. As I look back now, I realize Mrs. Horohoe had good reason to worry.

Until the time we were six years old, we were more or less confined to the block. We soon realized that if we stayed out of trouble, we could go anywhere. Our parents trusted us as long as they thought we were in a safe environment. Our parents always had a very narrow interpretation of safe environment. Catching butterflies to them was the safe environment. Our interpretation was much broader, only limited by death's door.

We started to get the itch to roam, like cubs wanting to leave the cave. Our parents loosened the reins a little and let the three of us wander in a nearby field to catch butterflies. We loved it. We competed with each other. The most prized butterfly was tiny, blue and much smaller than the plentiful white and the rarer yellow. The large orange and blacks were very common in those days. (This was long before the advent of the Gypsy Moth spray). We never used a net or anything resembling one. All we needed was the lid of a five-gallon tar can. The lids were easy to find because of the abundance of building material in our new neighborhood.

There were a large variety of butterflies, and they were plentiful. It's painful to think that some of those species are now extinct. I can remember the pleasure of stalking a big black butterfly with blue circles on its wings. I waited breathlessly for it to land. I had to make my approach with the utmost stealth. Creeping close with the lid in hand, I pounced, being careful not to crush it. I just used enough pressure to hold it against the soft grass. Oh, the summer air, the smell of the grass and the flowers, this definitely a time to catch butterflies.

The lid of the tar can reminds me of the unique time we grew up in. Up and down the block a whole new neighborhood was going up. Little did the builders realize that they were erecting a ghost town. The Great Depression was about to descend, causing these new homes, including those partially built, to stand empty and unfinished until 1940. A new ice age was about to hold us in a time lock. For roughly ten years, all construction in our neighborhood ceased.

While the building was still going on we set up a stand to sell lemonade to the Italian bricklayers. One of them talked us into pinching a bottle of wine from Phil's house to add to the lemonade. We did it, they drank it, and Phil got killed when his parents found out.

Then one day the only people left were the watches. These were the men hired to keep an eye on all the blocks of empty houses. Most of the people who had moved into the new homes soon lost them, as unemployment spread.

Once our parents set us free to catch butterflies, we adopted the life of the butterfly. We fluttered around the neighborhood, and what a neighborhood. Can you imagine what fun it was to have all those empty houses and construction sites to run around in?

The game that is called "man-hunt" today was called "ringa-leaveo" in our time. We played that for hours in the ghost town. I remember how frightened I was when being chased along a narrow foundation that was a little too high for my taste. Of course, you always had to be on the alert for the cry of "CHICKEE THE WATCHIE." When you heard that cry of alarm you immediately wished you were the fastest kid in the neighborhood. Out of nowhere a man appeared waving a piece of two-by-four and cursing you in Italian. The man bearing down on us was the watchman, hired to protect the property. Being chased was part of the excitement of growing up. Once in a while he would catch one of us. He would scare us, which would motivate us to run a little faster the next time we heard "CHICKEE."

Because of the construction coming to an abrupt halt, there were stacks of building material all about. Whenever we needed two-by-fours for building a clubhouse or stilts, we copped it from the stacks with a watchful eye for you-know-who. I remember even stilts had a season. For about two weeks every kid in the neighborhood walked around on stilts of various heights, depending on how much moxie he had.

As soon as we got tired of our stilts we turned to building scooters. These scooters were very simple to build. All you needed was one skate, a two-by-four about three feet long and one of those old wooden orange crates. You took the skate apart and placed two wheels on each end of the two-by-four. You then nailed the crate to the front of the board. In order to have something to hold on to while you scooted, you nailed two strips of wood across the top. They protruded at an angle, about six inches from either side.

After completing this operation, we hunted up another orange crate to make rubber band guns. In those days, the crate was made up of three frames, one on either end and one in the middle. We broke the frames loose and with a little sawing and chiseling, we produced about twelve rubber band guns. The little one-inch squares of linoleum that the gun shot could take your eye out at thirty feet. After we had our scooters and guns ready for action, we had our neighborhood war. Nobody lost an eye.

Shooting a game of marbles was a great sport. That was another season. There were a variety of different games you could play with marbles, but one was the most popular. Somebody said, "five up," then about four boys placed several marbles apiece inside a drawn dirt circle, known as "the pot". The brightest of the contestants yelled "LARRY!" That immediately designated him as the last shooter, which was the cat bird seat of marbles. The second quickest lad yelled, "NEXT TO LARRY" and so forth until the order of shooting was established.

The game had its own terminology, "rounds," "double rounds," "heist," "no heist," "killer," "globolers," "purees," "emmies," "fivers" and "tenners." By the end of the season I had managed to lose not only all of my marbles, but also a great many belonging to my brother, Bob. He was deadly. He attacked a pot as if his life was at stake. He had unbelievable concentration. I think he was the first person to be able to control a moving object with his mind. The marble he shot wouldn't dare stray from its appointed path. You know, I never saw Bob play golf or shoot pool, but if I ever had to face him, I would want a spot.

When I was cleaned out, I dipped into his supply. The only way the guys could get their marbles back from Bob was to play me. Occasionally, I paid the price. Bob did not take lightly to marble thieves. He was a strong believer in capital punishment. My saintly Mother, by placing her body between that raging maniac and me, prevented a punishment that definitely did not fit the crime.

Phil and I, with a lot of courage, occasionally borrowed Bob's B.B. gun. The Daisy pump gun provided a lot of sport. It was well worth the risk of Bob's wrath. Next door, our Jewish neighbors lost their house and left a large supply of Yiddish phonograph records in their basement. We carted the records into a nearby field for a skeet shoot. One fellow threw a record into the air, or rolled it on the ground, while the other guy took a pot shot at it.

B.B. guns were quite common in those days. Phil and I used to forage for empty soda bottles so that we could redeem them for the nickel deposit to purchase B.B.s. We knew of a doctor in the neighborhood who always had a supply of bottles in his garage. We foraged them. Five bottles got you a five pound bag of B.B.s. Kids were always eager to show you where a B.B. had hit them. It would leave a definite indentation in the skin. I regret to say that one boy did suffer minor eye damage.

When we were about nine, our parents could no longer keep track of us. We became free spirits. We soon discovered that our homes bordered an area composed of fifteen thousand acres that was originally purchased from the Keshawchquerin Indians in 1854. This land was composed of fertile salt marshes, verdant meadows adorned with wild flowers, and jungle-like thickets of scrub and vines dominated by a sea of cattails. Myrtle warblers, grasshopper sparrows, cottontail rabbits, ring-necked pheasants, horseshoe crabs and toads, are a small sampling of the animals that inhabited the area in and around Gerritsen Creek. It was a great area for small boys to camp, fish, dig, build fires, fly kites, catch butterflies, and live in our own world, free from the worriers.

Phil's father was a crack electrician, but was unemployed for several years. Just to keep himself busy, I guess, he built Phil and me two huge red and blue box-kites. Boy, did they fly! I never saw kites go higher. They were as steady as if they were nailed to the sky. And pull! If he had made them one inch bigger we would have been airborne. I remember once when Phil's cord broke, we chased that kite for about a half mile before it finally touched down just short of the millpond. I have built and flown a lot of kites since then, but I never came near the expertise of Mr. Phillips.

I remember one day he presented Phil and me with two bows and a bunch of arrows. Both had been handcrafted out of oak. I'm talking arrows. They penetrated an inch of wood. An old-fashioned tin can was butter at fifty yards. I have no doubt that one of our arrows would have gone clear through a person. The bows were so powerful we could send an arrow well over a hundred yards. I remember how my oldest brother Dick enjoyed using mine. When I look back now, I realize those bows were awesome. I wouldn't let my boys go near them today. Mr. Phillips was tops.

Frank Merrywell Never Lied

This is a sports story a little late in the telling, approximately 50 years late. I guess I'm the only surviving witness. The other eight or nine guys I'm pretty sure are dead. Bill Fox, the main character, is dead and I know Tom Yorkey is watching the all stars.

I figure you're a guy who appreciates a good sports story. The wingdinger about this story is that every word I write is true. You might not think of it as a wingdinger but believe it. I could put a lot of extra crap into it to hold your interest. What I do include is necessary background.

I have to fill you in about the main character. Bill Fox was a rare bird: honest, well read, trusting, innocent, intelligent, a code of values that Frank Merrywell wished he had. (For you kids, Frank Merrywell was the fictional all American boy.) Fox looked like Ted Williams, six-foot-one, square-shoulders, with black, tight, curly hair.

We were both nuts about college basketball. Back in 46-49, we followed St. Francis all over the City. After the games, we would try and catch the Friday night fights. In the mid-forties, the only place you could watch television was in the gin mills. The guys were stacked three deep at the bar, trying to focus on a six-inch screen. Remember Pep, Graziano, or Sugar Ray? Now that was boxing.

I'll never forget the first time I went into a bar with Bill. We had only been out of the service a few months. Remember how it was the custom to play the Star Spangled Banner just before the fight? As soon as they hit the first note, Bill was off his stool and at rigid attention. He was deadly serious and I was mortified. The other customers were staring at him. They didn't know if he was a wise guy or serious. To Bill the national anthem was the National Anthem.

Actually to get the real feel of the story, we'll start it in Montreal. It was our last year at St Francis, the summer of '49, and we wanted to make good use of what we knew would be our last long vacation.

Fox and I were *sans* car and had just a couple of hundred between us.

Luckily we discovered the American Youth Hostel, a hiking and bicycling club that had hostels all over the New England area and some in Canada. It fit right into our budget. We rented two old single-speed Schwinns in Greenwich Village and grabbed a train up to Montreal, with the bikes in baggage. From there we intended to pedal along the St. Laurence and then south through New England back to New York.

The only gear we had was carried in two old army packs, slung over the back wheels. The whole trip, including the rental of the bikes and food, cost us about a hundred and fifty bucks each. Our nightly lodgings cost us fifty cents and we threw a dollar a day away on food. We planned to be gone a month.

Upon debarking from the train, we immediately started peddling along the St Laurence. Bill had been with Patton and I had been with the 3rd Marine Division. We were definitely not in that kind of shape. We never trained for the trip, so the first couple of days could be described as hell on wheels or a real pain in the ass. Neither of us had ever owned a bike. If that trip were to be attempted today, we would train for at least a month on twelve speed bikes with all sorts of fancy equipment attached, and our credit cards.

As I mentioned, we had budgeted a dollar a day for food. Noontime we would stop at some small town to buy a loaf of bread, baloney and two quarts of milk. Then we'd be gone.

We would ride awhile into the country, pick a nice shady tree and collapse under it. A quart of milk, a baloney sandwich, a shady tree, and a good friend is happiness. Screw Patton and screw Iwo... God, we were free at last.

We stopped at a lot of beautiful towns. If you have seen one small, white church with its bell tower and steeple, you have seen most of the churches in New England. Picture riding down a country lane with your best friend, not knowing what is around the bend. Maybe you'll find a deep valley that will take your breath away, or a hell of a steep hill that will also take your breath away. We would fight that hill together and long remember it.

Most of the hostels were simply farmhouses or a house by the side of the road. I remember one farmer asked us to bring in his cows. When we got outside we laughed. How do you bring in a cow?

Neither one of us spoke cow.

Our nights were spent usually in private homes. AYH members were invited to use the hostel for a night's sleep and the kitchen facilities for breakfast in the morning. The rules were simple. You left the area cleaner than when you arrived, and you left something in the refrigerator. Our usual breakfast fare was pancakes, made with water and our syrup was melted brown sugar. Quite often we left the remains of what was in the pancake and sugar boxes.

One of the hostel stops was a cozy cottage situated in a quiet glen, off the main road. While Bill and I were eating our Spartan breakfast, this sweet, old lady kept rocking in her chair. She looked so huggable. She suggested we try her blueberry muffins and fresh butter. As she rocked, she kept insisting that we take as much as we wanted. They were very tasty and we scoffed them down. As we prepared to leave, the old bat-out-of-hell presented us with a bill for each muffin and pat of butter.

I have never trusted a sweet, old lady since. Bill and I had a good laugh at our expense and warned all hostlers heading her way that all the slickers weren't in the city.

We huffed and puffed up Mt. Washington and lost complete control coming down. We screamed past the cars going down, and I mean screamed. We thought we were goners.

Fox was an editor on the St. Francis Terrier; his one goal was being a sports writer. He loved baseball and insisted we take our gloves on the trip. On occasion, we would have a catch in the evening.

That spring Bill had failed to make the college team. I knew it still bugged him. He had played a lot of American Legion ball and loved the game.

The scale of fortune was about to be tipped. His moment in baseball folklore started when we reached Boston. We were staying in a small room in the Peabody Playhouse, just off the Charles. I remember the late actress Ruth Roman had her picture on the wall. I guess she got her start there.

We spent the morning walking around town, enjoying all the historic sights. We decided to go our separate ways for the afternoon, Fox to Fenway to watch the Red Sox and I was going to make a quick trip to Malden, the place of my birth. I had left for Brooklyn when I was two or three. I actually found my childhood home and even remembered the green cellar door that I slid down as a child.

We decided to meet back at the hostel about five. I got back to the room a little earlier than Bill and was standing by the window watching a boat race on the Charles. In he comes with a big grin on his face; you can almost see a canary protruding from his mouth. He had his glove under his arm. For a moment I thought he had caught a foul ball, but he wouldn't get that excited.

"How did you enjoy the game?"

"Sit down, you will never believe what happened." He had a full head of steam up and it looked like the boiler was about to blow.

"Get a load of this. I walk over to Fenway, but when I get there the place is empty, not a soul. Then I realize the team must be on the road. I'm about to leave, feeling pretty stupid, when I hear the crack of a bat inside the park. The gate was open so I kind of sidle in to see what's going on. There on the field, are about six or seven guys playing the field while they are waiting for their turn at bat. I'm standing there hoping and praying.

"Sure enough, some old timer playing short yells to me, 'hey kid, take left.' As quick as that, I'm standing under the green monster, the wall that will live in infamy. The tallest fence in baseball. I am playing left field in Fenway Park.

"I ask the fellow in center 'Who are these fellows?' He tells me they are all part of the Red Sox organization, but they couldn't go on the road for various reasons. It turns out one is a coach, another a sore-armed pitcher, a batboy playing second and the guy up at bat is Tom Yorkey himself, the owner of the club.

"After a while everybody has had a turn at bat but me. I didn't care; I thought it was great being on the field. All of a sudden Yorkey yells out at me, 'Come on in kid and take a few whacks.' In I trot... sore arm or not, this pitcher is major league. I feel the butterflies.

"Bill, he pitches and I hit eleven out of fifteen off the Green Monster. I mean, I was putting wood on it. I was leaning into it, but not trying to put it over the wall. It's like I'm shooting the ball out of a rifle, real hard line drives. After about the eighth, I glance at Yorkey. His mouth is so wide it's resting on his chest. Sore arm or not, that pitcher knew where my power was and he went for it."

Like you, I didn't believe his story for one second. It was certainly out of character. Frank Merrywell never lied. I wouldn't say I thought he was lying. I figured it was one tough hill too many. He was definitely out of his head. Now I start to wonder what they do with maniacs in Boston, and how am I going to get Bill Fox back to New York. He was returning my expression of horror with a look of ecstasy. It was obvious he believed what he was saying. He kept saying "honest" while I echoed "baloney." He was getting on my nerves.

Then he plays his ace. "Okay," he says, "come with me to Fenway tomorrow. Mr. Yorkey wants to take another look at me." But Bill is not finished. "Whatever you do, do not forget the camera. Mr. Yorkey is going to loan me a Red Sox uniform to try out in. I want a picture of me in that uniform to show that bum back at St Francis."

Well, Bill kept it up that whole evening, filling in the details of his adventure. I knew one thing; he believed it. Just like Thomas I had my doubts. I was going to believe after I focused in on that Red Sox uniform.

About two o'clock the next day, there we are in front of Fenway. This time there is an attendant at the gate. For some reason, he lets Fox in but not me. Bill quickly tells me, "Go around to the club house door in the parking lot. As soon as I get the uniform on, I'll dart out the door and you take my picture." Well, I went around to the clubhouse door and waited. I felt really foolish. It was like I was in Bill's dream.

Bingo!

The door opens and there stands the living truth. Teddy never looked better. Thomas focused in on one happy guy and became a believer. I shook his hand and wished him the best and told him I would meet him back at the hostel.

Now I'm caught up in it and excited as hell. While I waited in the room I thought how happy he must be. I mean, Bill loved baseball. If there ever was a guy who could appreciate this chance happening, it was he. You hear of being granted one wish. Just being close to a guy that got it was good enough for me. God, how good it must have felt to hit eleven out of fifteen off that wall.

Bill finally showed up. "Things hadn't been as great as the day before, but it was respectable. The pitcher pitched well but I hit my share. I didn't light up the scoreboard, but I wasn't embarrassed. Mr. Yorkey was very friendly and told me he might let me know in September. Because of my age (Bill was 24, two years fighting Hitler), he thought I might be a little too old to start in the minors. He said he saw a lot of baseball but yesterday was unreal. He gave me twenty dollars for my time. I think he might have thought I came down from Montreal to try out."

Bill was not dejected at all. He was looking forward to showing the coach the picture of "Ted".

I immediately suggested that we take advantage of his short career as a professional baseball player and shoot the twenty bucks on a good meal – enough of this dollar a day. I was quickly informed that the twenty was no longer legal tender but more of a memento of a great moment in sports.

Bill is long gone now, but he told me of a humorous incident that happened years ago. He did become a sports writer and one day found himself seated next to a player on a Texas team flight. He said he couldn't resist it. "I was with the Red Sox organization for a short time."

I imagine his wife or his children must still have the picture. His wife Nora told me that Bill once wrote a book. I know nothing about the book, but he might have written of his big day. The story is bizarre all right, but it's the truth. Frank Merrywell never lied.

Buried Treasure

"How long do you think it will take us to dig up this yard, Grandpa?"

"Well son, about as long as it takes us to finish the job. You don't seem to be in any hurry, so I guess it will take us awhile. You know I'm not in any hurry either. It's a real hot day so we'll take it slow. Let's just dig and talk."

"Grandpa, did you ever find buried treasure?"

"Son, it's funny you should ask that question. Yes, I found buried treasure. I found it while leaning on a shovel. This might sound odd to you, but I never had to dig for it."

I told him a story that happened during the Great Depression when I was a young man, not much older than he is now. There were no jobs, so the Government would give us forty bucks a month to work in the community. They called it the W.P.A. We built and repaired roads, laid miles of sewer pipe, created most of the parks we use today, and built the huge dams that supply our power.

We felt that the money given to us was charity. Sometimes we just couldn't get our hearts into the job. It was strange to see out of work lawyers, teachers, electricians, mathematicians and philosophers, all digging in the same hole.

I remember the spot and the very day I found the treasure. We were in a large hole down in Coney Island, and we were about ready to lay pipe. Every once in a while we'd take a break, just lean on our shovel and shoot the breeze. I heard some of the greatest stories while the handle of a shovel was supporting my body. Don't get me wrong, I did my share of digging in the thirties.

Since at that moment we were bonded by a common hole, Sam the English teacher said the scene reminded him of the way pirates dug for buried treasure. It didn't take much to get us started on what each guy would do with his share of the undiscovered treasure. In those days dreams were the staff of life.

Well you know what dreams are made of...loads of money, fame, power, big houses, big cars, beautiful woman, handsome children, and time to appreciate all the beautiful things in nature. While the guys talked, two things occurred to me. The first was that we all have the same hopeless desires. The second was that the oldest of us, called Pop by all, hadn't said a word. He's a strange duck, always laughing. He always seems to enjoy himself. He never finishes his lunch and always ends up giving it to the skinny guy who has a tough time with the shovel.

I couldn't resist, "Hey Pop what would you do if you discovered a buried treasure?"

He looks at me awhile then says, "Well, son, this will shock you. When I was a very young man I found a buried treasure. All that you men dream of, I have." He said it with such sincerity and openness that all attention focused on him. The hole was emptied of sound. We waited.

Pop put his shovel down and with both of his hands stretched out in front of him, in what seemed like a pleading gesture, he began to talk. He spoke with a sincerity that we were never aware he had. He spoke to us as if we were children.

"Why do you talk of happiness buried in dirt? Is your life so meaningless that you have to create a dream? You are the greatest and yet you make yourselves the poorest of God's creatures. Open your eyes and I will show you treasure beyond your wildest dreams.

"You are no longer children. You should by now understand that you are just a small piece of a body that, for each of you, has lost its value. You have chosen a particular point and place in time, assuming that you are the center of being. You want to draw the whole universe to your pedestal. Each of you has the same dream. How silly are your efforts to wish to be commended and honored by each other. The pedestal that you create is only large enough for the self. You cannot bring the treasure to your pedestal. You must go to the treasure.

"You seek possessions in vain. The selfish man will always remain barren. He can only wait to join the unremembered. If you sincerely want the buried treasure, I will give it to you. But, you must first understand the true meaning of treasure.

"Fred, our writer friend, will enjoy the fame of Hemingway. Sam will head the English department at Columbia University. If Charley, our mathematician wishes, he will be the originator of the theory of relativity. Amos, our learned councilor, will defend Dreyfus. That child, who won the honors, will be your child. Those beautiful roses, growing in the yard next door, are your roses.

"Do you wish to be that hawk that circles high above us in the heavens, or that graceful seagull that rides warm air currents from the nearby cliffs? You will be the swallow that darts over the meadow, or be proud of your colors as a cardinal. You will be the autumn mountain-side, the valley in spring bloom. You will be the first man to fly alone across the Atlantic. I will make you the richest man in the world.

"I see in your faces doubt, awe, and bewilderment. What I am saying is not the ravings of an old man. You can have all those things that I have offered you, this instant.

"You will also feel pain when a stranger is killed in an accident. You will know the grief of a parent of a retarded child. The hunger of the poorest man in the world will be yours. The terror of the small rabbit whom the hawk has picked as its victim, will be shared with you. You will feel the suffering of your neighbor who is dying, or your comrade being torn to pieces by shellfire. You will know the torment of someone's addiction. A piece of cardboard, on a cold winter night, will be your resting-place. You can have all those things that I have offered you, this instant.

"It all comes in one chest. All of you have this elusive treasure buried within you. If you love with all your heart, you have found the treasure. God is love and you are a part of him."

He looked his grandson as he leaned on his shovel. "Come on, son. Let's go have some lunch. Remember son, love and the world is yours."

The Kissing Bandit

"You're my last customer, Mr. Kias."

"Hey, Tony. Just trim the back and sides with the machine. How are the Italians doing? Do you think they'll take the Cup?"

"We're the best in Europe. You know, Mr. Kias, U.S. soccer is starting to take off. In California, they are packing them in. Next year, you wait and see. How are you doing? What's new with you?"

"I'll tell you what's new, Tony. It's one crazy story. You have got to keep it under your hairpiece. Promise?"

"Sure, Mr. Kias. You and me."

"At 7 o'clock tonight, I'm on my way to Louisville to a reunion of my old outfit. This morning I stop at the Bank and withdrew $500 bucks for my expenses and to do a little shopping in West New York. You know, outside of Miami, there are more Cubans in West New York than any other town in the U.S.? I bus it down to West NY and hop off in front of Modell's. I'm looking for a pair of sneakers. As I get off the bus I slap my back pocket for the feel of my $500 dollar wallet.

"Damn it! I had done it again. I realize my wallet is gone and it must have fallen on the seat of the bus. For the third time in thirty years I have left my wallet on the damn bus. Up until now the wallet had always been returned to me, *sans* money.

"My body vibrates with anger, panic and utter disgust. It's amazing how you can feel three different emotions at one time. I have the choice of two things: one, going over to the curb and throwing up, and then proceed to bang my head on the pavement or two, chase the bus down Burgenline Avenue.

"I take off at a speed that makes the roadrunner look like a slow sloth. My lungs are on fire and the old ticker is ready to blow, but I am closing the gap. I'm steadily gaining, thanks to the congested traffic. I finally run down the bus in the middle of the Avenue. I pound on the door until the bus driver reluctantly opens it. Bounding on the bus, I run to the back where I had sat. There is no wallet on, under, or in back of the seat.

"I think it would be kind of stupid, after my frenzied behavior, to ask if anybody has seen a wallet. I glance at the people who are now quietly staring at me. I had checked my pocket when originally boarding the bus. I am mad as hell and completely frustrated. Someone on this damn bus has my wallet."

Tony has stopped cutting my hair. He is now holding a dormant scissors and comb in either hand. He is on the bus with me.

"Just then the driver yells to me. 'Hey, Señor', as he holds up the wallet. A shabby old woman that I had rudely brushed past while running down the aisle has just given it to him.

"I rush to the front, grab the woman in my arms and give her one big hug and a kiss. God, I am in ecstasy. I tell her she had saved my life, and then I realize she has not understood a single word. It's time to celebrate. Despite her protest, I flip the wallet open to reward her, only to find it empty.

"To quote Bill Gates, 'Speed is God and time is the devil.' It is amazing how fast the brain works in a state of crises. My plan of operation is conceived at a speed that makes a Pentium look like an abacus.

"I feel I have no choice in what I must do. I am in a no-win confrontation with a busload of Cubans and a Cuban bus driver. I feel extremely helpless. I have to take control and right the wrong. In desperation I snatch the woman's pocketbook from her grasp and jump off the bus. I head down the yellow line at top speed with the bus driver in pursuit. After running two blocks, I realize the bus driver's hysterical screams had caused a posse to form behind him. I top my top speed.

"If I can only reach Hudson County Park where it borders the avenue, I can lose my pursuers in the thick wood. I know I need at least a hundred-yard lead. I have two things in my favor: the posse can not make time on the sidewalk because of the crowd of shoppers, and running on that yellow line through intersections takes the edge off the pleasure of the chase.

"God, there it was, the woods. I suddenly realize that there could be no sanctuary there. They would surround it and I would be trapped. They would beat the bush 'til I was caught. I could not stop. With a superhuman effort, heart pounding, fighting for air, I run and run. I suddenly realized how Frankenstein's big friend felt when all those bastards carrying torches were pursuing him.

"Finally, I crash out of the Park, into Fairview, hoping I have left my pursuers combing the woods. I continually glance back in search of the dreaded posse, keeping the pocketbook under my shirt. I run down Fairview Avenue. I feel as if I'm painted red and twenty feet tall. This is what nightmares are made of.

"Reaching my home, I go directly up to my room and rip open the pocketbook, only to find three bucks. There on the dresser, still in the Bank envelope, is my 500 bucks.

"Tony, you know what this means. I have to spend the rest of my life skirting West New York. They will always be looking for that stranger, the kissing purse-snatcher who can run like the wind."

Tony stood there stunned.

"Hey Tony, close your mouth. When are you going to cut my hair? I've got to get to Louisville. Keep cutting, Tony, and I'll tell you the true story. Everything I told you up until I opened my wallet on the bus was true. The truth is my wallet still contained the 500 bucks. I gave the old lady twenty bucks and stepped off the bus.

"NO, NO, TONY, NO SHAVE!"

The Lower Depths

I was standing on a rug of gum. Gum dating from 1904 to the present was lumped under my feet. I could feel the sweat penetrating my wash and wear. Sweat was about to drip from my chin, so I removed my tie and placed it in my breast pocket. I felt like I was standing in a Chicago holding pen with a herd of lethargic cattle.

As the train rushed in, we were blasted with hot air that is usually found on the wrong end of a flame-thrower. The only thing that saved me from being pushed on to the track was the excellent traction that the gum provided. The Brighton Express to Coney Island entered the 14th St. Station with its customary escorts, rats, the size of Cinderella's horses, running down the center of the track.

The train stopped and the car doors opened inches from my face. I could sense that a mass of uncontrolled energy was about to explode behind me. It was comparable to standing on the track in front of the starting gate at a racetrack, as the horses were about to lunge forth. Inside the train, the exiting passengers were gathering to make their break. The rush hour crowd on the platform, with their weight on their toes, was ready to surge. The doors opened displaying a scene that resembled cars compacted in a junkyard. There was a short pause, amid cries of pain and curses, as passengers fought their way out on to the platform. Those standing in the doorways would not step out, whereby permitting these poor souls to exit. This was acceptable etiquette on the Brighton, where Calcutta rules hold sway.

Everyone managed to escape but one old gentleman, who ran out of time as he attempted to clear the door. The closing of the doors acted as a starter gun. I immediately felt the pressure of a Coney Island breaker on my back as I was catapulted into the car, compressed into the wall of flesh. The old gentleman gave up his struggle as he became one with me. He was our prisoner. The doors struggled to close upon bodies that continued the assault, some more in, some more out.

It reminded me of the bloody angle at Gettysburg. Those who were not quite in, left the car, as toothpaste leaves the tube. It was a moment that showed what a person was made of. There was the quitter, who was always looking down as he withdrew; as if he had dropped something. Then there was the last man to get on, whom everybody hated. The last man had to be made of the right stuff. He had to be a no good son-of-a-bitch, who didn't care whose ribs he broke or whose toes he mashed. While he causes all sorts of pain and injury, he has to put on an injured look and constantly cry out, "excuse me," or, "pardon me." These words have completely lost their meaning on the Brighton. Once the door closes he immediately attempts to bond by saying "Whew," which is supposed to mean, "I'm just like you, and isn't it nice we all made it."

By the time the door closes I find myself crushed against a pole in the center of the car. I glance up at the dead overhead fan and think bad thoughts. The man next to me is reading a newspaper. This requires a special skill. Before entering the train he has folded his Times in a manner that somewhat resembles an accordion, permitting him to turn pages that are the width of a newspaper column. This method of folding is not easily learned and must be passed down from father to son.

The man in back of me, whose chin is resting on my shoulder, seems to lean toward a heavy garlic sauce. The man whose face is buried in my chest tends to drool. The little old man who had become our prisoner has disappeared. I feel something soft under my feet.

As a new arrival, I immediately join the other passengers who are already caught up in the subway syndrome; sometimes known as subway hibernation. Everyone wears the same expression of intense discomfort; at the same time creating an image of being the sole occupant of the car. Eye contact or any form of recognition is unacceptable. A threatening defensive look is acceptable if you grow tired of the fat guy leaning on you.

On the other side of the narrow pole there is a small man that has all the appearance of being a gypsy. He is wearing a small fedora over black curls and a gold earring. His face is dark and swarthy; around his neck a red bandana.

I always thought that before I said anything, I first passed it over a few dendrites. Not this time. "HEY!" just came out of me. The gypsy hand was unclasping a little black ladies pocketbook.

His response was just as fast. "Miss your pocketbook is open."

She responded with a, "thank you, sir." She meant it, as she snapped her purse closed. The pickpocket accepted her thanks with a friendly smile.

I was flabbergasted at his quick response. It was over in far less than a second. There was no doubt he was a professional. He had not taken her money; he had not committed a crime. I was left with my "HEY!" still hanging in the air. I was waiting and sure enough our eyes locked. His eyes spoke hatred and loathing and yet there was a trace of a smile. He had that coolness that his profession called for.

The train continued, stop after stop. As my station was drawing near, I pushed and shoved to get near the door. I did not feel comfortable in this man's presence. While doing this, I noticed the gypsy was imitating my example and also making a move toward the door. I was frightened; this guy did not like to lose.

As we fought our way out the door together, I felt his body brush against mine. I cringed expecting a knife between my ribs. For a moment we were almost nose-to-nose. His evil smile appeared once more, as he whispered to me, "thanks." Instinctively, I replied, "you're welcome."

It wasn't until I was home, changing into summer shorts and looking forward to a cool Manhattan, that I realized that I had told the gypsy that he was welcome to my wallet.

Multiple Choice

My writing is like my singing. It's my nerve, not my talent that is to be admired. I have never signed the Webster agreement. I have never even met the man. I spell to a distant drum. It's so much easier for me to tell a story over a cup of coffee than to put it down in grammatical form. I have a long history of poor writing, a history that came very close to ruining my life. You think I jest, or exaggerate? You say, "How can that be?" The only reason for the existence of the word processor is due to the power of my prayer.

When I say I have never passed a spelling test in my life, I do not exaggerate. In grammar school, I saw more red 20's and 30's on my test papers than I can block. The thorn on my other side was my childish handwriting, which would leave me in tears.

When I was in the service, I found myself painfully inept when I attempted to write home. My output was so meager that my family threatened to have the Red Cross on my back. Thank God they kept writing to me. Receiving a letter in the service could only be compared to mouth-to-mouth resuscitation.

While I was attending college, I was keenly sensitive that my spelling, handwriting and composition were far below college standards. The essay question spelled my doom. Studying a subject in order to be prepared for an exam was always a futile exercise. When I gazed at an essay question, what I knew of the subject was secondary. I attempted to hand in a blue book that had the minimum of handwriting and the simplest words. I was majoring in Philosophy and Sociology, and although I always enjoyed studying both subjects and knew them well, this was my secret.

If I knew my subject cold or lukewarm, it made no matter. I was guaranteed a C. Along with my thousand C's, my transcript shows two F's, four D's, one B and no A's. My two F's were in Money & Banking and Mathematics of Finance. They were the only courses offered one summer; I found them excruciatingly boring, especially when compared to a beautiful blond fellow student that I could not put on a high enough pedestal.

After three years, I was warned that if I didn't pull A's, to up my quality point index in my senior year, I was history. I gave it my best shot- the old college try, but to no avail. I was history.

I wasn't quite history. For the next twenty-seven years I attended St. Francis at night. When the final marks were posted, I found that I had inadvertently been sitting in the wrong room the entire semester. Other nights, I knowingly attended the wrong class while other students stared at me. Some nights I never found my class and just wandered the halls. If ever a college had a ghost wandering the halls at night, it was St. Francis.

I beat them out of tuition, but how I suffered in those nightmares! I awoke from my dream each morning, exhausted and extremely frustrated. I knew there was no vacation to look forward to. I was damned. My nights at the College were as real as my days. This, undoubtedly, was not an unusual dream to have due to the circumstances. But how long, oh Lord? How long? Of course, I thought often of returning but I knew there was no solution to my problem. I didn't want to get caught up in that mess again. When I had left, I was either on the verge of a breakdown or having one.

*   *   *

On my fiftieth birthday my family gave me, as a present, a weekend retreat. They do that to fathers when they want to get rid of them. I always enjoyed a retreat. Each of us should be entitled to at least one retreat a year. I think the greatest measure of a successful life is to be able to sit in an empty room or under a tree and enjoy solitude. I always felt sorry for a person who found their life boring, constantly looking for distraction. As preventive medicine is for the body, a retreat is for the soul. It provides that opportunity to make peace with oneself

The retreat house was situated on a hill and had a beautiful view of the Hudson. The West Point Cadets always held their Christmas retreat there. The rooms were comfortable and the guests I met, at dinner, were amiable. We spent the early part of each day at a church service, after which there would be lectures on various subjects. The teaching focused on various needs of a spiritual healing. Most of the day you spent alone, to meditate, or to do some spiritual reading. The last day of the retreat, the subject of the teaching was "Healing of Past Memories." I sat in the pew and sardonically laughed to myself. Oh, to change the past, what a wonderful world this would be. Ah, to sleep, to miss a class, to have that episode in my life never to have happened. But, no. "Life is a drag, and then you die."

It was the custom after the service, those that wished to be prayed over, went to a certain area and there would be a laying on of hands and a prayer request for a healing. "I believe, Lord, help my unbelief." I got up and stood in line. I asked the prayer team to ask God for the unique healing that only was possible for Him. I asked for a memory to be removed from my brain. The cutting out without leaving a scar. I gave no details.

Immediately after the service, as I was retiring to my room, I paused in front of my door. A gentleman in clerical garb about my own age was passing by. Up until that moment I had not noticed him at the retreat. As he smiled at me I asked him if he was one of the fellows giving the retreat. He said no, he was a Franciscan Brother and just another poor soul making the retreat. I told him I had attended a Franciscan college in Brooklyn. Within moments we were aware that we had attended St. Francis together. We had never known each other or exchanged words while there, but we did remember each other.

I remembered him as a scholar, who was always in the company of Dr. Clemens, one of the sociology professors. He remembered me hanging around with Bill Fox, the Editor of the Terrier, up at the Greasy Spoon. I invited him into my room to discuss the old days on Butler Street and to reminisce about our student years in the "Closet." The College had only five classrooms. I told him how I had never graduated, and briefly related to him my painful experience with my grades and the horrible aftermath. I told him how I had just prayed for a healing of past memories. It was the first time I had ever spoke of my dilemma.

Without a moment's pause, without any word of sympathy or question, he said to me, "You're healed! You're going back to St. Francis and graduate."

I said to myself, Wow, I always thought this guy was a little strange, but aloud I said, "No way."

"You're healed," he repeated.

I smiled at him, "Impossible."

"You're healed. I have the gift of healing. You're healed, no question."

Again, I thought to myself, what do I do with this guy? He is deadly serious, but aloud explained why it would be impossible. "One, nothing has changed. I still have the same problem today that I tried to overcome during my school years. Two, I'm married and have seven children and no money for tuition for Dad. Three, I have been out of school for twenty-seven years, and I feel I should never had been there in the first place."

"You're healed! I told you, I have the gift of healing." He said this in a very soft, loving, but determined, voice.

I started to feel guilty, as if I was denying the existence of God. It was exasperating; he was so damn sure. He got up and left and I never saw him again. I later tried to locate him, only to find out that he died in Mexico while serving as a missionary. I had never met a man with such faith; my healing was a fact to him.

I put the episode out of my mind and the following day, I went back to work in the bank. That afternoon we were called to attend a meeting; a talk was to be given by a woman representing the Focus Program. I had never heard of it. The gist of the talk was for members of the bank to further their education. It was obvious that her talk was pointed toward education in the banking field, but she didn't say that in words. The bank would pick up all tuition fees. She appeared as a very friendly person, so jokingly I asked her if the bank would pick up the tab for a Philosophy degree. She said she couldn't see why they wouldn't.

About two weeks later, after work, I found myself walking into St. Francis. They had moved from Butler Street to a beautiful new building on Remsen Street, in the heart of downtown Brooklyn. When the space race was on, the government sprung for some big bucks and the College rebuilt and expanded. The "Closet" had turned into Brooklyn's UCLA. Well, not quite.

I felt very old and ill at ease as I walked into the office of the President. I thought I was entering the Dean's office. The President was a stout, friendly looking guy. He popped from his desk and shook my hand, putting me completely at ease. I mean, he was exceptionally friendly. There wasn't a phony bone in him. I told him about attending the college in '46, my dilemma, and that I now wished to complete my studies. I naturally didn't mention attending night school. I asked him for the bottom line as far as obtaining my degree. He asked his secretary to hit the archives and bring back my transcript.

While waiting for the secretary's return, he filled me in on the many changes that had taken place in the school since '46. The enrollment had grown from 500 to 3,000. The Index, a list of books that students were forbidden to read, was a laughable memory.

The secretary returned with my transcript and left. As the President looked at it, I felt as if I was standing before God as he reviewed my sins. All of a sudden he broke out laughing and called for his secretary to return. "Hey, Charlie, look at this. They took half a credit off this guy for not attending a graduation ceremony of the class ahead of him. If we tried that they would burn down the building."

I remembered the loss of half a credit seemed quite normal to me.

My clothes kept dropping off as he kept studying the transcript. Finally he looked up, "Here is the deal. If you get two A's in two three-point courses, you can have your degree in Philosophy. You have enough credits for a degree in Philosophy or Sociology."

Well that was great. Back to square one. I accepted his offer and thanked him and left. I figured I might as well learn something I can use. I signed up for two courses that ran back to back at night, during June, July and August. Child Psychology was to start in mid-June and Psychology of the Adolescent, was to end at the close of August. Why was I doing this? My senior year was still in my mind, as fresh as last night. My best shot was already fired and scored as a miss. It was going to be a painful summer. Every night I would be riding the subway from Brooklyn to the Port Authority in Manhattan and then grabbing a bus to Jersey. Not a night patrol, but close.

It was almost May and I had two months to prepare. I knew I wasn't the sharpest tool in the shed, so I had to make use of every minute. I got hold of a Child Psychology textbook from a young friend who had recently graduated. I devoured the book and, just to be sure, I chewed the cud and devoured it again, underlining about every word. After reading it the third time, the Swiss psychologist, Jean Piaget and I are like this (). He was the man to know. I went deep into Piaget, a tough guy to read. I became Piaget. I was obsessed. I was afraid to walk away from the book. What the hell, one more time. No, more. No, more.

Come June my potential to know child psychology has been filled to the brim, and packed down. I have done all I can. I know in my heart that I haven't accomplished anything because those blue test books are my real nemesis. Come mid-June, it's time to enter my nightmare. Everybody is going to wonder what Pop is doing in the class. Is he going to make an ass out of himself? What the hell, it's another adventure. What has that Franciscan wrought? "I believe, Lord, help my unbelief." At the very least I'll get fresh material for my nightmare. I'll be wandering through a new building.

I work down in Greenwich Village so it's a short haul to Remsen Street, which is just over the bridge. The first night, I arrive early and I'm sitting in class checking out all those bright ambitious kids going to night school. Bingo! The professor came bounding into the class. A little fat Italian guy, throwing his briefcase on the desk and spieling, "My name is John Amoro. I'm a professor of Psychology at Iona College. I'm here just for the summer. I give two exams during the semester. These exams will be comprised of two, one hundred multiple-choice questions. One will be your midterm mark and the other will be used to base your final mark. I will also require a term paper, which will make up the final third. The reason I give multiple choice questions is that, using an answer key, I find it easier to mark."

I sat there spellbound. Multiple choice test. You didn't see too many of those in the old days. A piece of strawberry short cake. That Franciscan Brother has clout.

The fun began. I participated more in that class than I did in all the courses I had ever taken, rolled into one. I could have been elected President of the Know-It-All Society. His midterm tests were murder for everybody but me. I nailed it.

I was cracking up. The straight "A" students brought him up on departmental charges. They said his testing method did not permit them to demonstrate their true knowledge of the subject. They didn't know that he was just a character in a miracle; their beef was with the Healer. The Department backed the Professor. The kids started to believe I was a scholar with terrific insight on the questions to be asked on the final. It was as if I had died and came back smart.

I had a gray goatee, which made for a wonderful disguise. A straight "A" would come up to me and ask, "Mr. Kias, what do you think he is going to ask on the final?" I had no idea what he was going to ask. I rubbed my goatee, gave her a charitable look, and replied, "Look for the key words on each page." It wasn't much help but it was as profound as I get. What was happening to me? I was going through a drastic personality change. My self-esteem was hitting the roof.

The term paper was a pleasure to write. I had the necessary weapons: a typewriter and a dictionary to defeat my old opponents. I gave him Piaget until he must have thought I was Swiss. The whole situation was unreal. The man with the pointed laurel was basking in sudden scholarship.

What I enjoyed the most was class participation. When I was speaking, I said to myself, what fun! They're actually hanging on my every word.

Just for the heck of it one day, I asked the Professor, "Is it possible to change one's personality?"

He said, "If you break the handle off a hammer and replace it, and then break the head off and replace it, what has happened to the old hammer, and what do you have now?"

I told him, "A born-again hammer." I guess I answered my own question.

I had received an "A", using only one lobe. To me an "A" isn't an "A"; it's a miracle. But reality started rearing its ugly head. One "A" does not make a summer; it meant nothing. I had been incredibly lucky. I had three days off before I went back to class for Psychology of the Adolescent. I had been following the same study routine for this subject as I had for the previous one. When Dad went to school, Dad went to school. I was really impressing my children.

I sat in the class the first night and started to look for familiar faces. Bingo! The Professor bounded into the room, throwing his briefcase on the desk and says, "My name is John Amoro, I teach psychology at Iona College. I give two multiple choice exams." Etc.etc.

It had never occurred to me that he was going to teach the second course. What I had first thought would be a horrible experience, turned out to be my summer of extreme content.

The last day of class my buddy John suggested I pursue a Masters Degree in psychology. I was sorely tempted to explain to him that I was far from an "A" student, and that I had viewed the whole summer as an episode from the Twilight Zone. I felt that when I left the building, he was going to disappear along with the College.

By September I had my degree, the Franciscan was in Mexico, the Professor back at Iona, the President of the College dead, and as the good Brother said, "You are healed." The memory had been cut out; there is no scar. I dream no more. Life is not a drag, and you don't die. Praise the Lord.

Nose Knows

We were attending the fiftieth reunion of the 3rd Marine Division in the Grand Ballroom at the Hyatt in New York. It was actually the first occasion since World War II that I had ever attended a Marine Corps affair. I had always made it a point to stay clear of any Marine Corps reunion. Believe me, I had good reason. Why I went on this occasion I'll never know. Time does not heal old wounds.

It was a formal affair; everyone looked great. The orchestra was playing Stardust and my Honey was singing softly in my ear. In the middle of her song she suddenly stopped singing.

"Bill, ever since we started dancing there has been a man staring at you. He can't take his eyes off you, and he doesn't look happy. In fact he looks like he is going to explode. Bill, my God, he is barreling people over and heading this way."

I whispered with trepidation, "Honey, I'm not going to look, just tell me, does he have red hair and a enormous nose?"

"No it isn't red, it's gray. Your right about the nose, it's unbelievable. That's what caught my eye. How did you know?"

"That's Nose."

"My God, that's Nose. I remember the story. Bill, he is barreling people over, he is heading for us."

"Honey, grab your wrap. We're getting out of here fast."

As our cab pulled away from the curb I looked out the rear window. For a moment I thought we were safe away. Not so; staring at me through the side window was an elderly gentleman in a tux, who appeared to be frothing at the mouth. For a guy of seventy, Nose could really move. He was now pounding on the window and so I ordered the cabby to step on it. Nose for a moment kept pace, his proboscis pressed to the window, screaming in a language that I had long since thought dead. Just before he blew a gasket and went sprawling, he shouted, "I'll get you Kias, you're the last one!"

I thought to myself, with a guy like Nose against you, the Japs never stood a chance. Nose still has that temper.

I guess you're wondering why this man would be out of sorts after fifty years away from the playing field. This story is from another place and time, so don't be too hard on us.

Some of us thought of it as a joke, others as a good deed. It really didn't make any difference. The hidden motivation for our weird behavior was absolute boredom. I have seen so-called cowards risk their lives and get killed because of boredom.

At the time I was quartered in a tent on Guam with five insane men. Our only method of survival was to live "off the wall." The only contact we had with that other world was the mail from home. It was the only reminder that there was something to hope for. Maybe there was another world somewhere.

At mail call, the company clerk stood in the circle, surrounded by the platoon, as he called off the names on the letters. Your name never sounded sweeter. Gathering our mail, we would retire to our tents.

Absolute silence fell over the tent as we sat on our sacks, drinking deeply of home. Not everyone enjoyed this blessed respite. Nose lay on his sack with his hands clasped behind his head, staring at the overhead. Our Squad Leader was never known to get mail. He had spent his entire youth in a Catholic orphanage, St. John's Home for Boys on Staten Island. In 1940, when he turned seventeen, he joined the Corps.

He received the Silver Star while serving with the Second Raider Battalion on Guadalcanal. He was a warrior and enjoyed killing. I guess you would say war was his game. Nose had his faults. He wasn't quite right and had a hell of a temper. I think he left half his deck on the Canal. He wasn't the safest guy to bed down with. When sleeping in the boondocks he always kept a bare bayonet near his head. There was only one way to wake him and that was gingerly. We always grabbed the bayonet before we rousted him. Let's say he wasn't a hugger: you gave him a lot of room.

He was the kind of guy, you wouldn't invite to dinner, but he would be the guest of honor on any patrol. Nose always reminded me of Kipling's "Tommy".

As I have mentioned, he had a nose and a half. The Sarge was mighty proud of his huge and beautiful proboscis. It was like those postcards you see of the Matterhorn; it dominated his face, an eye catcher, worthy of admiration.

After digesting our mail we exchanged the high points, keeping the love life news to a minimum. It was a standing joke, and threat, that the first guy home, was going to hit on all the other guy's girls.

Gunner suggested we send one man down to collect the mail, instead of all of us having to make that hike down to the Headquarters tent. He volunteered to be the mailman and took off.

When he returned with the mail, to our great surprise, he dropped a letter on Nose's sack. Nose was not in the tent at the time. We stared at each other in shock. Nose got a letter? Who? Where? What? We bolted to his sack.

Gunner stopped us before we could get our hands on it. "Take it easy, I wrote it. It's about time that poor bastard got some mail. The Sarge saved our ass on the Canal and nobody gives a shit about him."

"What do you mean, you wrote him a letter?" we chorused.

"Well it's not exactly from me. I wrote it, but I made it look like it's from some dame. I used a canceled stamp. How do you guys feel reading your mail while he is lying on his sack? I can't take it anymore!"

Gaskin asked, "What the hell are you going to do after he reads it?"

Little Morgal had a big grin on his face, "I think you made it, Gunner. This rates a Section 8. You lucky bastard. You're out of here."

Gunner smiled, "Don't worry I got it all worked out. Here he comes!"

Nose made his entrance, we buried our heads in our mail, and no one dared look up.

"What the hell is this? I got a letter?" No one answers him. Our heads are still down. I thought, what in God's name has Gunner done? Nose was long gone around the bend; can Gunner be far behind?

He started reading, sitting on the edge of his sack. Suddenly he threw his head back, his arms above his head, his feet going into the air.

"Listen to this," the Nose chuckled. "'Dear Johnny, I saw your name in the Leatherneck Magazine and what you did on Guadalcanal. The Marine Corps was kind enough to give me your address.'" Nose then proceeded to read every word to us.

Gunner was the only college guy in the tent and could really blow smoke. He was the master of the snow job. All we kept saying was "Wow!" We all figured "Wow" was a pretty harmless remark. It was very embarrassing. I half hoped he would wise up and yet afraid he would. It was musk ox stance time.

Nose was absolutely crazy about the letter. A new man was born right before our eyes. There was a light on his countenance that we had never seen.

Gunner expected to spread a little joy but not ecstasy. The letter had a life of its own. The bride of Frankenstein had risen and had clasped Nose to her bosom. What had Gunner wrought! What a mess!

Nose was the Sergeant of the Guard that night. We took advantage of his absence to question Gunner on how he was going to keep us out of a mass grave. You just don't fool with Nose. Nose does not take prisoners; there was no quarter at the orphanage.

Gunner never lost his cool. "Here is the plan. It took me a while, but it's really very simple. The address on that envelope belongs to my buddy's little sister. My buddy lives on a farm next to mine. Every time his sister gets a letter from Nose, Art is going to forward it to me under separate cover. I'll answer the letters. Nose isn't that quick, he will never realize what's going on. After Iwo, if he is still around, I'll send him a "Dear John." He has nothing over here to keep him going. He has about lost it. What the hell?"

The bored bastards that we were, agreed it would be interesting. We all realized that if Nose stumbled on the truth he wouldn't hesitate lobbing a grenade into our tent.

All the while we were preparing for the campaign, Nose kept getting letters. By now Gunner has created damn near a real person. Nose is in love with Gunner.

Well you know what happens. Old Nose wants her picture. Gunner's buddy Art provides him with a picture of some living doll. Big mistake! We had our out, and Gunner blew it. He should have given him a picture of the homeliest girl in town. Nose nails the picture of this beautiful creature to the tent post for all of us to admire. It finally dawns on us that the babe is a young Hollywood starlet. We all live in fear that someone is going to walk into the tent and recognize her.

He talked about Mary constantly. She started to have a real existence, and became flesh and blood. We actually made suggestions about what Nose should say to Mary. I swear some of us got a crush on her. She was a knockout. I told you we were insane.

Well, the day finally came, the ships were loaded and we were ready to board. We fell out on the road, with the kitchen sink on our backs, for the long march down to the harbor. Everybody stood outside the tent but Nose. He finally came out with a letter in his hand.

"Fellows, I finally did it. I just proposed to Mary." Would you believe we all shook his hand? Puzzled, we looked at Gunner, wondering if joint congratulations were in order. All of a sudden a horrible thought hit me, what if Gunner is killed? Who would write the "Dear John"?

The last time I saw Nose and Gunner, they were being carried aboard a hospital ship heading for Hawaii. Gunner never made it.

That's why I changed my name to Monks and never went to a reunion.

Nose knows.

The Not So Good Samaritan

It was about a week before Christmas, some twenty years ago. I was about to leave my home for work when my ten-year-old son presented me with a twenty-dollar bill. He asked me to purchase a blender for his Mother as a Christmas gift. I knew the money was hard earned; he got up every morning at five a.m. to deliver newspapers. He had his first route when he was eight. He was an old eight. There was an apple that fell very far from the tree.

I placed his bill in my wallet along with the three singles that carried me through the day and headed over to that wonderful town, New York City.

I was freezing as I walked down Sixth Avenue. It was a miserable, cold, overcast morning; the temperature was in the twenties. I fought the war in the Marine Corps just to avoid cold weather. To me, cold weather is very painful.

I was about to make the turn to head down to Fifth and Thirteenth Street, when I spotted a guy lying on the sidewalk. His body was pressed closely to the side of a large office building. He looked like hell. His hair was extremely long and matted, with a black beard to match. I guess you could say he was in his prime, about thirty. What clothes he wore were filthy and well worn. Surprisingly, his shirt was open from the neck to the navel, with nothing on his feet. His flesh was as filthy as his clothes. The poor fellow's head was resting on his shoes and a small bundle. A couple of slabs of cardboard served as his bed, but he slept like that old rock. The constant movement of the morning herd didn't bother him one bit. I wondered how he lasted the bitter cold night in such a naked condition; this poor homeless chap might be dead.

Just looking at him made me shiver. I couldn't pass him by without easing my conscience. I reached into my wallet and removed a single, and attempted to stick it into his partially closed fist. I really didn't want to touch him; he looked as if he was crawling. As I placed the bill in his hand, his eyes opened and glanced at me and then into his hand. A look of pleasure and surprise lit up his face as he beheld my son's twenty dollar bill. He looked up at me and what he saw in my face will puzzle him to his dying day. I looked at his firm grip and all I could say was "Merry Christmas" as I staggered around the corner, a man broke by grief and lack of largess.

Well, I'll tell you, I never laughed any hardier than I did for the next half block. Any passerby would have thought I had had my morning fix. I had just given a poor soul twenty bucks and my account was not going to be credited.

When I got home I told my son what a generous boy he was, but he didn't buy it. He insisted I get all the credit, and he, his blender.

The next day, the weather was still frigid as I passed by the exact same spot, where the man I now own, was once again sleeping. My man is still half-naked. This time a warm quilt has been added to the scene. I figure somebody from the apartment house across the street must have donated it, when they spotted the desperate straits he was in.

Now here is the kicker, he used it, only to rest his head. He had not just thrown himself haphazardly down on the sidewalk. No way. He had chosen his place of repose with great care. He was lying along side of a six-foot grating that was attached to the side of the building. This grating was covering a fan that was exhausting tons of hot air on the sweating unfortunate. Cold was not his problem; he was probably the warmest guy in New York, and I the dumbest.

Twenty dollars. Really the story was worth twenty bucks. I still laugh when I think of the expressions on our faces when we both looked at that twenty. Who knows, I might have mistakenly saved his soul and renewed his faith in his fellow man.

Out of the Closet

She provided very little information on her application outside of giving her address. She lived in a luxurious apartment house across from the bank. I opened her account about three years ago. She deposited a huge sum in new thousand-dollar bills, but showed no interest in the rate she would be getting. I cannot describe her beauty to you, no more than I could describe color to a blind man. She was beauty, I mean ethereal. She was of what Wordsworth spoke.

There are some people who never take a smile off their faces, but it's a false smile that tends to irritate. My beauty's smile always called for an echo. It was a caress that had to be returned. She was in the full bloom of celestial youth, a form divine. She entered the bank as if carried by a warm breeze, floating more than walking, her dainty feet barely touching the ground.

I have to admit even though I was a married man, when she entered the bank, this withered sunflower paid homage. All my attempts at gathering more information from her were unsuccessful. I knew her for three years but she always remained a damsel of mystery. Always alone, she never mentioned friends or family. The only thing I found out about her was that she was never home at night.

Each day she came in, sat at my desk, and we chatted. What I think attracted her to my desk was the conglomeration of pictures I had of my children. After a short time she inquired about each child by name, as if she knew them. She appeared to be bright but had no interest in current events, not only no interest but also no knowledge. Outside of talking about my children, I found it difficult making small talk. She was completely unaware of anything that was appearing in the news media. How could a person, who appeared so friendly, live the life of a recluse? She never spoke of her nightlife.

I asked her if she had ever been married. I couldn't believe a woman of her rare beauty had escaped the Romeos of New York.

"My life does not call for a marriage. I would find it extremely inconvenient. I really never think of it. One mission dominates my whole life and that can only be accomplished at night. In fact, the only people I ever talk to are in this bank. I have no time to socialize."

I thought, this classy babe is a nut. Could she be a lady of the evening? No, too genteel. Only spoke to people in the bank? I had worked in the Village for thirty years, I thought I had met them all. I'm a nosy guy and usually successful in getting my customers to share the story of their lives. Each day as she sat at my desk, I delicately tried to delve into her life and background.

"Where do you work? Are you in show biz? What do you do for fun?" I had to know.

"I can't tell you what I do. It's very confidential. I'm constantly on the move from dusk to dawn. I shouldn't tell you this, Bill, but it is undercover. I live a very unusual life, it is not dull."

Every attempt to probe into her life, no matter how subtle, she would delicately parry. The conversation always ended up with us discussing the lives of my children.

One day she let her guard down. I noticed she had left a package on my desk after one of our chats. It was long after she left before I noticed it. I called her apartment.

"This is Bill over in the bank. You left your package on my desk. I'll drop it off at your home after three."

"Oh no, Bill, that is not necessary. I'll be right over."

I insisted, "It will be no trouble. I have to pass your place on my way home."

"Oh, that is so nice of you. I'll be in my bedroom, but I'll leave my apartment door open. Bill, I hate to delay you, just put the package on a table. It's awful nice of you to go to this trouble."

Did she need sleep that bad? I was determined to find out what she did at night. This might turn out to be quite an adventure. Life in the Village had made me wary of setups. Was I walking into something I might regret?

When three o'clock came I picked up her package. It was heavy as hell. I finally got it up on my shoulder and left the bank. It was a short walk; she lived almost facing the branch. It turned out she had the penthouse apartment, a very classy place.

Sure enough the door was open. I knocked and entered into a large room. What immediately caught my eye, and boggled my mind was it's strange contents. Every flat surface in the room, even the mantle, was stacked with glass jars, hundreds of glass jars, each one containing coins. Kennedy's, Susan B. Anthony's, Indian pennies, coins from every foreign land filled the jars. The room put our coin vault to shame. There was hardly a place to stand. The jars were stacked three high even along the walls. The only other thing in the room was a pair of gossamer wings hanging on a hook in the corner.

It suddenly dawned on me what I had on my shoulder was coin. This is why the woman came to the bank every day, she collected coin. I also suddenly realized, she had always left the branch with a package. How did she manage that weight?

"Bill, is that you?" she asked.

"Yes, you have a nice apartment. I hope you have a strong floor."

"What you see, Bill, will be our little secret. You will have to excuse me, but it's very important that I get sufficient sleep."

I managed to find a bare spot on a table to place her package and turned to leave. In my bewildered state I mistakenly opened the wrong door. As I turned the knob, the door flew open and I was buried in a mound of baby teeth that had cascaded out of the closet.

Yes Virginia.

Where Were You? ...Out!

I recall a group of us looking up at a street light, as it reflected off the falling flakes. We stood there with our mouths open, catching the snow, not an easy trick.

Eventually a car, with its chains clattering in the night, would slow down to make a turn. The back bumpers in those days were not streamlined but jutted out, allowing for a good firm grip. As the car slowed, we would all take a bellywop at the bumper. Some guys got it, some missed, but the fellows who missed still had a chance to grab the back rudders of the sleds that made the hitch. Sometimes we would be three abreast, or a chain of sleds 3 or 4 long. It was fun and exciting, we moved along at a fast clip. It wasn't for the faint of heart. If bad luck had its way, you would hit stretch of dry pavement, sparks would fly and you would feel as if your arms were about to leave their sockets. You would hold on as long as you could, hoping that you could ride out the dry spot.

If the driver became aware of the chain he would either stop and chase us, or, if he were a good sport, he would take evasive action, and try and snap us off. A fast corner would do the trick, and we ended up in a snow bank.

We picked ourselves up, had a good laugh, and got ready for the next hitch. Sometimes we lost a sled in the action and spent the rest of the evening on a friend's back. Nine out of ten sleds in those days were Flexible Flyers. They were sturdy and got most of us through our youth.

After hitching a couple of hours we were frozen stiff. We headed for my cellar to thaw out. I can still smell and feel the heat that came out of that old coal-burning furnace. We dried our gloves on it as we huddled around it and shivered.

Those old furnaces had two drawbacks. If we forgot to stoke and bank them at night it would be murder getting out of bed with the fire out. The other problem was lugging the ash cans up the cellar stairs and putting them out on the sidewalk. My brothers and I did not look forward to ash day.

You can imagine how grateful the guys on the Department of Sanitation were when the neighborhood switched to oil.

About ten days after the Christmas holidays, the neighbors took down their trees and put them out in front of their homes so the garbage men could include them in their pickup. We shuddered when we thought of a beautiful Christmas tree being stuffed into a garbage truck. Thanks to the kids in the neighborhood, very few trees ever saw the back of that truck. We devised a much more fitting end to the object that had brought so much pleasure during the holidays. As soon as the trees started showing up in front of the houses, the gathering began. We scrounged the neighborhood that whole week, amassing a stockpile of trees. It was highly competitive.

Each gang of kids strove to have the biggest pile. It was a common sight to see two boys lugging a tree down the middle of the street. We stashed them in secret hideaways, preferably in somebody's back yard. We were always acutely aware of tree thieves. All trees were fair game, no matter where you found them, even in somebody's back yard. When you were carrying you had to be wary of treejackers, the big guys. If you don't know why boys put such an effort into gathering a bunch of Christmas trees, than you never saw one burn.

Finally, when we had scrounged out the neighborhood, we started getting giddy with anticipation. Late in the afternoon we moved them out to a desolate area in the grassland. We had about a thousand acres of barren land surrounding our neighborhood. When night fell we were ready. The trees were as dry as that proverbial bone, yet still filled with pine tar, begging to light up the night.

The trees were stacked into a huge pile, made up of about fifty trees. Get the picture: night, dark, cold, in the middle of nowhere, not a parent to be seen-we were ready.

With fiendish grins we attacked the pile from all directions with our matches. At first there was heard a low crackling that was being emitted from each individual puff of smoke, then small orange flames started to appear on the circumference of the pile, and then those Christmas trees did what only they could do. In seconds an orange ball of flame, the size of a house, exploded from inside the pile. The heat was so intense, your lungs burned and your skin pained.

From the summit of this mountain of fire, a huge shower of sparks was sucked high into the dark sky. The sheer beauty and horror of it forbade you to move. There was only the fire and the black night.

The tree that one-week before was used to demonstrate God's love had also the potential to show us vividly hell's fire. It appeared too awesome to be in our midst. We felt we had created something too diabolical to grasp, an evil genie springing forth from the depths.

In a short while it was all over and night was blacker. How could someone put that into a garbage truck? There remained on the ground only the charred skeletons. I remember for many years they lay over the landscape marking all the Christmases past. It reminded me of the Great Plains, when they were strewn with the bones of the buffalo, after our forefathers had almost exterminated them.

To this day, when I visit a home at Christmas and the host asks, "What do you think of our tree?" I always think of it burning, but I just say, "Beautiful."

*   *   *

"HEY, BILL, YOU COMING OUT?" None of the guys ever thought of using a doorbell. I think the reason we did this was to keep a safe distance from the parents. They were not to be trusted. They asked too many questions, like, "Where are you going?" When I got outside there was old Phil, redheaded, freckled face, short pants, no shirt, wearing a beat up pair of Keds. On his knees, he wore those badges of an active life, two scabs. He was clutching a hammer in one hand and a bag of nails in the other.

"Hey, Phil, what's up?"

He smiled, "How would you like to build a raft down at the millpond and sail it down the creek, out into the bay?" The bay was the Atlantic Ocean.

"Wow, what a great idea. Wait one minute and don't talk so loud."

There are some things that parents are too old to understand. We knew they would prefer thinking we were out catching butterflies. Not that we had anything against catching butterflies.

His nerve was only exceeded by Phil's imagination. I quickly disappeared into the cellar. In seconds I appeared with my Father's hammer and pockets filled with nails. We made a hasty retreat out of my alley before I could get a call back on Dad's hammer.

When we arrived at the pond, we had no trouble gathering up driftwood along the shore. Our building strategy leaned more to haste than to stability or beauty. All we knew about shipbuilding was that wood floated; you needed a place to sit and oars to get you where you wanted to go. We built a raft that any two ten-year-old boys would be proud of. We poled off and, in a short time; we were out in the middle of the creek. With the help of our paddles and mainly the tide we made fairly good headway. The creek was about three hundred yards wide, and about thirty feet deep in the channel. It was about a mile out to the bay. I remember a four mast Spanish training ship had once dropped anchor right in our channel; I saw it with my own eyes. I often wondered why she had sailed up into that desolate area of water. I think it was a hell of a mistake. I figured the poor navigator thought he was entering Sheepshead Bay, a body of water that opened about a mile further down the coast.

Phil and I were out on the raft about an hour, moving at a good clip, about to leave the creek and head into the open bay. My instinct to survive made me conscious of two facts that had a strong relationship to each other: one was that most of the wood we had used was waterlogged, and our raft was turning into a submarine. It was not riding as high out of the water as when we first started. The second fact was that I had not won any swimming medals lately. I informed the redhead of the seaworthiness of our vessel and my lack of swimming prowess. He quickly attempted to put my mind at ease by informing me that he could swim, meaning good enough for both of us. His confidence in the raft had not wavered. This guy was made out of Huck Finn stuff.

As we reached the opening of the bay, the wind and the water kicked up. We were in complete agreement that we were in deep trouble and that this might be the end of us. As the bay opened in front of us, it became obvious that we were running out of shoreline to make a landfall. We soon realized that altering course on a raft that was going with the tide, was one tough job. After a terrific and frightening struggle, we just barely made it ashore. When I got home that evening, late for supper, my Mother was ready to go around the bend. She used her favorite expression, "I'm going to tear the skin off of you." I always tried to picture my self without skin. I condensed my adventure into that one word that saves mothers so much needless worry. "Out, just out". Dad's hammer is still at the bottom of the Creek.

*   *   *

Phil was a pilot during the war. God should have made him a bird, he lived to fly. I think he flew every weekend of his life. When he came home after the war, we flew over that same inlet. He had this old biplane, dual-control, with open cockpits. It really wasn't his. He had a summer job spraying crops out on Long Island. It was my first flight and Phil had no mercy. To Phil, fun and danger were synonyms. We skimmed over the old millpond, and then up, up, and away. I felt like I was in a World War I fighter plane, one of those flying coffins. I mean this crate was old. All that crate needed was those twin Vickers that Phil could fire through the propeller at the Baron, and a Lewis for me to nail those specks, diving out of the sun.

Phil had one flying weakness that he managed to conceal from the Air Corps and the "Bouche". He was the only guy I ever knew that, when he looked into the sun had a sneezing fit. I had shellfish. Phil had the sun.

He insisted I take the stick for a while. When I did I had a strange feeling that I was parked, till I noticed the wings were flapping. I didn't know wings did that and I didn't want to know. I logged about five minutes; just long enough to show him I too was made of the right stuff. I was amazed that I was flying that crate. I would have much preferred being back on that flimsy raft, fighting the current.

Phil, who had spent his life as a test pilot and aircraft designer, died in his sleep at fifty-six.

I never forgave him.

To My Readers

I hope that my sharing of life's memoirs with you has been an enjoyable experience. This is my first adventure with the creative Muse of short stories and it has been a most delightful undertaking.

I invite you to write and share your thoughts on these stories with me. I promise to respond and thank you for your kind attention. As a novice author, your comments are invaluable in shaping my future writings.

My e-mail: bsnaw@aol.com

Or write to me in care of my publisher, who will forward your letter: John James Company, 79 Worth Street, New York, NY 10013.

Best wishes,
Bill Monks